MURDER
IN THE
MANOR

An addictive crime mystery full of twists

ROY LEWIS

Arnold Landon Mysteries Book 2

Originally published as
Most Cunning Workmen

Revised edition 2021
Joffe Books, London
www.joffebooks.com

First published in Great Britain in 1984
as *Most Cunning Workmen*

ISBN: 978-1-78931-808-1

Most cunnynge woorkemen theare weare prepared,
Withe spediest ordynaunce for eauery thynge,
Nothynge expedyent was theare oughtis spared
That to the purpose myght bee assystynge;
One thynge (chieflye) this was the hynderynge,
The woorkefolke for lacke of goode ouerseers
Loytered the tyme, lyke false tryfelers.

They weare thus manye, á thousande (at the leaste),
That thearon weare woorkeynge still daye by daye,
Their paymentes contynued, their labours decreaste,
For welneare one haulfe did noughtis els but playe.
If they had trulye done that in them laye
By so longe space as they weare tryfelynge,
At his fall had beene lyttle to dooynge.

William Forrest,
The History of Grisild the Second

CHAPTER ONE

1

The darkness was complete.

It held an ancient, close, musty odour, the secret breathlessness of a room that had been closed for centuries. The flagstones were soft with an undisturbed dust, untouched by the decay and death that had occurred beyond the darkened walls. Over a distance of time the darkness had awaited the light of day again, living hands, a closer contact with the realities that moved above.

The darkness was complete, but not the silence. It was broken from time to time as it had always been broken, by whispers, by words, by sibilant sounds that were siphoned down into the heavy darkness, sounds of another world, a younger world, a new world.

No one had come near; no one had probed the stone, but someone would. It was bound to happen eventually, and light would return, and humanity. It was only a matter of time. So the heavy darkness waited, patiently, for the stone to be moved and for the violence to come.

2

For Arnold Landon, arriving at Oakham Manor had been like crossing a bridge made of mist.

He had felt as though it was necessary to tread softly, lest a shimmering image disappear for ever. The warmth under the trees was unlike anything he had previously known in the northern hills; the heat of the midday sun was softly filtered by tall sycamores and the moss-grown stone of the gatepost was grey-green, warm to his touch.

He had walked the length of the curving drive, gravel crunching under his feet, through bursting azalea, wild rhododendron and Himalayan poppy. Across to his left he had caught glimpses of the unruffled blue placidity of the lake and when the drive had straightened and the rhododendron thinned he had seen manicured green lawns, shaded by copper beeches through which the light breeze shouldered, whispering soft excuses. His mind filled with romantic images flitting from the past: young ladies in white dresses twirling nineteenth-century parasols; gentlemen with frock coats and high stocks; teacups and silver salvers, black Labrador dogs and town talk, society gossip, guns, grouse and the surrounding, spreading Northumberland hills.

'Wouldn't have thought it was the way to spend your holiday,' the Senior Planning Officer had grumbled. 'Burying yourself in a library.'

The Senior Planning Officer was aware that Arnold had been brought up in the Yorkshire Dales but had now been captivated by the sweep and grandeur of the Northumberland hinterland, where crags, coast, hills and castles conspired to produce an unmatchable, for Arnold, scene.

'*We're* going to Scarborough,' the Senior Planning Officer had announced. He always went to Scarborough, to escape from his wife's cooking. Arnold was constrained by no such demands and normally was able to indulge his passion for exploring the high fells. Library research at Oakham Manor was different, he had to admit, as the Senior Planning Officer sniffed and mournfully extolled the delights of Scarborough.

But Arnold knew the Senior Planning Officer would have been impressed had he seen the Manor. The beauty of the old manor house had swept over Arnold and would surely have touched the Senior Planning Officer with its warm stone, mullioned windows, gables and turrets and pendants and buttresses. Arnold had marvelled over the gargoyle-adorned east wing and the rebuilt, cunningly masoned west front. Oakham Manor was smug and powerful in its strength and style, arrogant and proud of its heritage. It had seen centuries and families and its day had not yet come. Its heart had been constructed by craftsmen, and fire, decay and five hundred years had not humbled it. It was serene, with gentle meadows that ignored with an elderly complacency the motorway that roared a few miles to the east of the house.

A bridge of mist protected it from the harsh reality of the world outside; Arnold had crossed it in his mind and it shimmered there, a barrier against the standards of the present. Arnold hoped it would remain a protection against the men who would be coming, the people who would determine the future of Oakham Manor. The manor house could doze confidently in the afternoon sun, but Arnold had work to do and, for the manor house, prayers to say.

He whispered his prayers and got on with his work.

* * *

4

It was not an unpleasant task, cataloguing the books and papers for the Northumberland Heritage Society. They had written to him — 'The price of infamy,' the Senior Planning Officer had grumbled, still unforgiving over the Old Barn affair which had splashed Arnold's name all over the northern newspapers — and explained the problem to him. Priceless manuscripts, books, private papers could be lost during the next few years. They had little time, less expertise in areas such as Arnold's passion. Could he, *would* he, help them . . . ?

'In your own time,' the Senior Planning Officer had said as he caressed a stomach savaged by his wife's leaden soufflé. 'The department's still not recovered from your last foray into Cumbria and I want you to keep your head down. What you do during your leave, of course, is up to you.' Scarborough, he added, was a better option.

Arnold had decided to help the Northumberland Heritage Society. He had then discovered that, true to the ways of the world, members of the Society, concerned though they might be at what they described as the 'coming rape of Oakham', had found nevertheless that the summer months and family commitments demanded their presence in France, the Balearics and Bridlington. So Arnold was alone in the library as the sun filtered through the mullioned windows. The drifting dust was his only company.

He did not mind the isolation. It allowed him to work at his own pace, uninterrupted. It enabled him to break off from time to time to wander the dark corners of the library, run his hand over the carved oaken shelves, caress the polished surfaces of the massive tables and admire their almost invisible joints. It allowed him to get to know the room in which he was working, and think of the men who had built it, as well as work on the manuscripts.

The papers and books comprised a fine collection. The Vallance family, owners of Oakham, had had an eye for the important and valuable in terms of collections. The person mainly responsible, Peter Vallance, father of the present owner, had been a man of taste. Arnold sensed this rather than understood it: his own appreciations were for timber and stone, but he felt that Peter Vallance had had the same understanding of manuscripts. He would have liked to have met him, so that they could have traded appreciations. Arnold could have told him that there were fifteenth-century carvings in this library, blending into the dark-timbered room; in return he would have learned much about the provenance of some of these books.

For some of the papers intrigued him. As he carried on cataloguing, his mind often drifted to one in particular and its dog Latin which spoke of the construction of the original buildings on which Oakham Manor had arisen in the fourteenth century. It intrigued him by its language and by its mystery.

Latebras et diverticula.

The words were never far from his mind, teasing him, puzzling him as the bees hummed under the roof and the time slipped by in the cool library room, and he worked his way through crumbling, brown, dust-laden, lawyer-odoured conveyances.

* * *

The Heritage Society had fixed him up with a room at an inn some six miles distant and negotiated his presence at Oakham with the owner. He had worked at the Manor for several days before he met her.

He thought of her as a girl, immediately, even though she was about twenty-five years of age. Perhaps it was the fact of her height — she was only a little over five feet tall in her stubbornly flat shoes. Or it may have been the elfin quality of her features, the slimness of her body, or even the innocent candour of her wide-spaced brown eyes. She was dressed in jeans and sweater, and the directness with which she addressed him as she stood staring at him from the library doorway had all the honesty and curiosity of a child.

'Who are you?'

'Arnold Landon.'

'What are you doing here?'

'I'm doing some work for the Heritage Society. They got the owner's permission for me to catalogue and investigate the books and papers that are stored here.'

'Are you qualified to do it?'

'Hardly,' Arnold admitted after a momentary hesitation.

'But *they* think so?' the girl pressed.

'I don't suppose I'd be here otherwise.'

'So what are your qualifications?' Somewhat disturbed by her directness, Arnold sat back in his chair and folded his arms. 'I work for the Planning Department at Morpeth. I . . . I'm interested in mediaeval matters — particularly building, wood, stone . . .'

'But my father's papers—'

'Old papers are concerned far more with land and buildings than people,' Arnold interrupted. 'Property stays; people don't.' He hesitated. 'Your *father's* papers?'

'That's right.'

'*You* are the owner of Oakham Manor?'

She glanced at him, and as she walked forward into the room a hint of sudden anger glinted in her brown eyes. 'That's a moot point, as the lawyers say.' She gestured past him to the papers stacked on the table. 'You've read those?'

'Most of them.'

'Then you'll know about the Vallance family. About its waywardness, its black sheep, its essentially masculine attitude towards inheritance—'

'Laws tend to be masculine,' Arnold said, 'like lawmakers and lawgivers. As for black sheep . . . they exist in all families. I had an uncle who became a railroad detective in the United States at the turn of the century.'

She stared at him. 'What's black sheep about that?'

'He'd absconded because of a third poaching offence, in Yorkshire.'

'Even so—'

'He'd seduced the wife of the magistrate who'd been trying the case. When the magistrate was at church. It seemed a good idea to leave.'

'I believe it.' She laughed suddenly. It was a light, pleasant sound that seemed to change the room, making it younger and happier. 'America always was a haven for the disinherited, the disenchanted and the dissolute.'

'He didn't drink.'

'Did he have time?'

Arnold grinned. 'I don't know, but he met Jesse James.'

The girl perched herself on the edge of the table, one leg swinging. 'Anyway, if you've read those conveyances you'll know a fair bit about the family.'

'It's a bit confusing . . .'

'Let me unravel it for you. Oakham Manor was established here in fourteen-twenty. Prior to that it was in use as an abbey.'

'*Latebras et diverticula*,' Arnold murmured.

'What?'

'Nothing.'

'There was some kind of squabble going on around that time, or maybe the king, Henry the Sixth, was putting some kind of pressure on.'

'The way powerful people tend to do.'

'That's right.' She paused for a moment, glancing vaguely around the room. 'That is right. Big people, they always feel they have the right to push little people around, don't they? I mean, business people, the kind who have big corporate empires behind them, they think they can just come in and tear down traditions and history . . .'

'I'm not quite certain what you're talking about,' Arnold said.

'It doesn't matter,' she said, as the anger in her eyes faded. 'I was talking about the founding of the Manor, wasn't I? Not visiting all my troubles on you. As I was saying, there was an abbey here but the good monks moved out in fourteen-twenty. Not too far. They just moved along up the hill, not more than about half a mile. The old ruins are still there—'

'Walbur Abbey?'

'That's the place. Anyway, when they moved out the old abbey was taken over by the Wolfard family. It's from that family that my father traced his descent. We go way back, you see.'

'Evidently.'

'It was Thomas Wolfard who moved in and drew up the plans and the agreements to rebuild that part of the abbey that had fallen down. He did various bits and pieces, set up a tower, and generally refurbished the old place.'

'And that was how the manor house came into being?'

'Just like that. But there was a problem.'

'How do you mean?'

'Problem for me, that is.' She wrinkled her nose, and thought for a moment. 'If things had been different, if the timing had been different . . . You see, there were two Wolfards. Brothers. Thomas and William. Thomas was the elder. He moved into the place; started rebuilding it. The trouble was, he didn't live long enough.'

'How do you mean?'

'He had a son, born after his death. But before the son was born, William took over Oakham. The result is, the line, the ownership of Oakham, is traced through William, not Thomas.'

'That's important?'

'Very.' The girl smiled ruefully. 'Over the next four hundred years there was a lot going on but the Wolfards clung on to what they had pretty grimly. And in the nineteenth century they were home safe, except by then the line had changed through cousins and what have you — some of whom took the Wolfard name, but eventually that was dropped. And it finally came down to my grandfather, or so we thought.'

'How do you mean?'

'James Vallance — my grandfather — thought his title was secure. He had a passion for genealogy, and he was

9

eager to strengthen the information available regarding the Vallance link to the Wolfards. He started making inquiries. It was a mistake. It threw up another claimant.'

Arnold blinked. 'His title was put in doubt?'

The girl nodded; dark hair tumbled across her eyes and she brushed back the lock with an impatient hand. 'That's right. It seems from the records that in the sixteenth century there was a kind of slip-up. A Vallance had moved into the succession as a cousin and taken over Oakham Manor, but there was another branch of the family, tracing its ancestry to William Wolfard, which had gone to the States, to Virginia. And my grandfather's research showed that his line was traceable only to *Thomas* Wolfard's family.'

'The branch which had lost title to William Wolfard's clan?'

'Precisely.' The girl pulled a face. 'My grandfather was an honest man. He got in touch with the other branch. They were called Castle. A sum of money changed hands. The matter was agreeably settled. The old man stayed on, my father — Peter Vallance — succeeded, and when he died about eight months ago, Oakham Manor fell to me. But—'

The girl scratched her nose and shrugged. 'The Castle family crawled back out of the woodwork, in the form of Andrew McNeil Castle. And I'm now in the middle of litigation. So, like I said, my ownership of Oakham Manor is a moot point.'

She stood up suddenly, scraping back the chair, and moved around the table, brooding over the piles of papers and books, unsettled, clearly disturbed by her own account of the situation she found herself in.

Arnold realized now why she had failed to recall her agreement with the Heritage Society; she would have had more important things on her mind. And it would be why she had not been at the Manor these last few days, leaving Arnold to be received by the three servants who were in residence. 'I don't think any of this appears in the papers I've looked at,' he said.

The girl shook her head. 'No, I suppose not. The relevant conveyances and legal documents will be with my solicitors in London. They've been arguing the toss for ages. I hope it gets resolved in the not-too-distant future.'

Arnold frowned, looked around him at the materials on which he had spent the last five days. He was vaguely puzzled. 'This litigation, Miss . . . er . . .'

'My name is Antonia Vallance,' the girl said. 'But I'm known as Tina. It's less of a mouthful.'

'Ah, yes . . . er . . . Miss Vallance,' Arnold replied awkwardly. 'But this litigation, and its outcome . . . the Heritage Society is making the assumption that you will fail, and the Manor will revert to Mr Castle?'

Tina Vallance stared at him, puzzled. Then her brow cleared. 'You mean they think all this stuff here might get shipped back to the States by Andrew Castle? No, no, that's not the position.' She glanced around her, taking in the tall ceiling, the dark gleaming shelves of books. 'No, you've got to remember that Oakham Manor and its acreage is an anachronism. Our family is not a wealthy one, not by modern standards. There are two farms, but they only scrape by. Some of the land was sold off thirty years ago by my father, to pay death duties when my grandfather died. I'm in debt now, as my father was. No, what's happened is that an American company has an option to purchase the land, which they got from my father about five years ago.'

Arnold shivered, looked around the splendid library, and frowned. 'What would an American company want with Oakham Manor?'

'Nothing, at that time. My father knew the managing director — he was an American Anglophile who had been at school with my father. It was all really by way of a loan, the purchase of the option — to help tide my father over difficult financial times.'

'But situations changed?'

Tina Vallance smiled ruefully. 'You can say that again. About two years ago my father's friend lost out in his own

11

personal battles: his company got taken over by a conglomerate. There was some talk of my father buying back the
option, but he couldn't afford the price the new financial
wizards put on it, and my father's friend was helpless. He
died, shortly before my father. And the option was trans-
ferred to the conglomerate. And, in the meantime, enter left
the wicked uncle Andrew McNeil Castle, right on cue. He
sees the deal as a way of picking up a nice bit of cash, if he
can prove title to Oakham—'

'You mean Mr Castle wouldn't want to live here at the
Manor?' Arnold asked.

Tina Vallance shook her head. 'He'd take his money and
run like hell. Back to the States, I think.'

A sadness had descended upon Arnold. He understood
now the anxiety of the Heritage Society: the twin ogres of an
unsympathetic heir and an international American company
were threatening materials they would consider part of a local
heritage. He sighed. 'That's all very sad.'

Tina Vallance jutted her lower lip and shrugged. 'I suppose my uncle has a point of view. He doesn't really know
the Manor — he's never lived here, wasn't brought up at
Oakham the way I was. He doesn't know the Manor, hasn't
felt its presence when darkness falls and the meadows kind of
glow down by the river, you know what I mean? He doesn't
understand the musty smell of the place, its own solid *life*
that's meant a history rooted in a distant past. For him it's
nothing but a windfall, something he can convert into cash,
to make his later life more than comfortable. Do you know
what I mean?'

A fierceness had crept into her tone; she was taking Andrew
Castle's point of view, trying to see the situation through his
eyes, but she was unconvinced by the justice of it all, and she
was hurt and scared and annoyed too. Arnold understood very
well. Gently he said, 'Maybe this American company won't
take up the option. After all, what could they use it for?'

The angry light died in her brown eyes to be replaced
by a half-veiled frustration. 'I don't know; I wish I did. I've

tried to talk to the man who runs the company, but it's like fighting cotton wool — all these bland, smooth young men at the other end of the phone, with soft assurances, gentle persuasion in their tones. But no answers. All I do know is that they are interested, and have some ideas about the place. But I've no doubt whatsoever it will be a far cry from what I would have done with Oakham — and would still try to do, if I had the chance. But that means in any case I'll have to wait for a court decision in my favour.'

'When do you expect a decision?'

She laughed; it was a brittle sound that emphasized the feeling of rancour that was clearly shading her day. 'You tell me. It's been months already. Time seems to mean nothing to lawyers — I sometimes think they forget they are dealing with people at all. It all comes down to papers tied with pink ribbon. But it *must* be soon now. There's another hearing scheduled for next week. I just hope . . .'

Arnold watched her sympathetically as her voice faded, and she looked down at her hands. He could sense she was near to tears; he guessed she would not allow him to see them. She straightened her shoulders, looked up at him. 'Anyway, you'll have time enough, I think, to get your work done for the Society.'

'I hope so. And . . . I'm sorry, Miss Vallance.'

'And you might even get to learn before you leave what is to be the final destiny of Oakham Manor and its farms.' She folded her arms, walked across the room and stood at the mullioned window, staring down into the courtyard. 'Who knows?' she mused, 'You might even have the opportunity to get across to the company some of your own sense of the history of the place.'

* * *

'I don't understand.'

She looked back over her shoulder, and then made a jerking motion of her head. 'Come over here.'

13

Obediently Arnold scuffed back his chair, rose and walked across to join her at the window. She was very small beside his tall, thin frame, her head barely reaching his shoulder. He looked past her, down into the cobbled courtyard where elegant carriages and magnificent horses had once rattled and clattered their way from stables to entrance for the owners of Oakham Manor. Now, in the bright pool of sunlight there was crowded the arrogant, gleaming opulence of three sky-blue United States registered cars. Arnold experienced an odd feeling of sickness in his stomach: the churning of unpleasant anticipation.

'There it is,' Tina Vallance said, making no attempt to hide the bitterness in her voice.

'The cars—'

'The *circus*,' she corrected him. 'The outriders, the guardians, the first troops in the invasion.'

'The company?' Arnold asked, surprised.

'Exactly.' She looked up at him, her smile hard-edged. 'I was asked if I would agree, for a not inconsiderable sum, to their using the Manor for a few days. It would help them make up their minds about the option. It would help *me* get to meet the man who runs the company.'

Arnold looked down at the offensive sky-blue glitter in the courtyard. 'What's the name of this company?' he asked.

Tina Vallance moved away from him, towards the door. 'It's an international company, but big in the States, where it all started. Curious people, the Americans; so thick-skinned, so humourless. The company's called Computer Analysis Design Systems Inc. Can you believe it? Their mnemonic is splattered all over their stationery. CADS Inc. Could anyone other than our American cousins be so brash, or insensitive, as to try to take over Oakham Manor and all it stands for, with a company name like that?'

She watched the cavalcade from the safety of her own room for a little while. Two more cars arrived. Squeezing in behind the others, they disgorged dark-suited young men who seemed to be possessed of precisely the same nervous energy that resulted in loud voices, quick pacing, sharp, decisive movements of the hands, as though they were indulging in some private war with the elements about them: sunshine, light, old stone, age, history.

They were puppets away from their normal stage; jerky in unfamiliar surroundings; uncoordinated in an atmosphere beyond their comprehension. Or was she merely being fanciful in her anxiety and fears?

The movement continued, leather suitcases being carried into the house, discussions in the courtyard, the Oakham servants drafted in for the visit being subjected to long, detailed instructions. The north wing was now commandeered, but Tina was safe in her own room with her part of the house sealed off behind the oaken door. She knew she need see little of these intruders; she knew also she would have to nerve herself to meet them, to greet them, to get to know and understand them — before they took Oakham Manor away from her . . . or from Andrew Castle.

So she stayed there behind her screened window and watched, and in a little while she realized that much of the activity in fact seemed to revolve around a quiet epicentre of four men, three who remained close together, as though their proximity to each other gave them an added strength, and a fourth who was with them yet not of them, in some oddly indefinable way. They spoke little, but were the prime movers, the central nervous system of the minor operation being undertaken down below, yet in themselves they were not individual, they were part of a whole.

Except the one man, who stood a little to one side, saying nothing, watching with a slightly bored air, and surprisingly more concerned, it seemed, with his surroundings than with the activity. He raised his grey head from time to time as though sniffing at the wind; she could not see his face but she had the feeling that he would have sharp grey eyes that pierced every corner of the courtyard, seeking out every mortared stone, checking every weakness, weighing up in an adversarial balance every recognizable strength.

It was only when he moved out of sight and into the Manor that she realized he was older than the other three men. It made her also realize that he had drawn her attention in a way the others had not done.

They were of a mould. Tall, broad-shouldered, dark-suited, confident, aggressive, *certain* of themselves. They did not swagger like bullies; they displayed no qualities of *braggadocio*; even so, they had emanations of sureness, a knowledge that a snap of the mental fingers would be translated into action, an understanding and use of a power structure that was centralized upon their existence. Something left the three men when the older man entered the Manor; the relaxation was not visible but it was palpable, nevertheless, and one of them, the heaviest of the three, lit a cigarette and drew upon it with what seemed a heartfelt relief. And as the activity around them diminished so, one by one, they moved out of the courtyard, into the house.

The one who was finally left seemed to hesitate on the steps of the house. He looked about him with an air of interest as though he was really seeing the place for the first time now that the bustle was all but over. She watched him as he stood there, tall, cleanlimbed as all young American men thought they were, and he suddenly surprised her by raising a scrubbed face to her window. Their eyes met, glances locked, and his smile was involuntary. Tina Vallance did not smile. When he went inside, she checked her hair, her mouth, her eyes and her emotions, and then she went downstairs to beard her adversaries in their den.

Tina's choler arose, unreasonably, when she found that the small room at the foot of the grand staircase that swept into the hallway had already been commandeered and turned into an office complete with three word processors and something that looked to her eyes like a mini-computer. It was all too foreign, too efficient and too swift. She raised her chin and her courage and swept past the bustle to head for the drawing room, the splendid, deeply carpeted, panelled and logfired room that had been made for crystal wine glasses, classic profiles and inconsequential conversation.

It now housed three men, young, different, alien in these surroundings, and a fourth who sprawled in one of the deep armchairs with a brandy glass in his hand.

He rose when she entered and set down the glass.

His charm was in his smile; the fact that it was practised made no difference. It touched her and if he was seventy years old he could still reach out to a woman as he reached out to Tina. She could think of nothing to say, except the obvious.

'I'm Tina Vallance.'

The eyes were not grey and asset-stripping at all in their qualities: they were a soft hazel which gave the impression of caring and, through experience, knowing. He came forward, extending his hand. 'And I'm John Torrance.'

'You head the company,' Tina heard herself say in surprise.

Gravely he replied, 'I do admit to being the major CAD. I once had a sense of humour, you see.'

She had the panicked feeling he could look into her soul and read what lay there. She stared at him, hastily summoning the defences of critical review. She saw a man who was below middle height but lean-fleshed, whipcord in his build. His hair was iron-grey but still thick, worn short at the back, and his face was deeply tanned, even more deeply lined, cicatrices of experience running from the base of his nose to his mouth, and setting up cracks and patterns in the skin about his eyes. His mouth was dangerous: its soft malleability could, she suspected, change into a rigid strength at a moment, a reflection of the character of the man himself. He could be — and had been — a man for all men and, as she caught the twinkle in those soft hazel eyes, for more than a few women too. But now, perhaps, he was an observer, a man who controlled by virtue of experience, knowledge and understanding.

And ruthlessness, she warned herself, fighting the captivation.

'I'm delighted to have the opportunity of meeting you,' John Torrance was saying, still holding her hand in his, firmly but gently.

'I'm surprised,' Tina replied. 'I'd received the impression you had no desire to come face to face.'

'Ah, you misunderstand,' he said, shaking his narrow head with the air of one who is misunderstood by so many. 'I have — how can I describe it? — conscientious aides. They feel they know what is best for me. They protect me. They are enthusiastic, and concerned. But, as on this occasion, they are also from time to time prone to error.'

Three men laughed at the joke. John Torrance still held her hand and her glance: she saw a deep amusement in the old man's eyes, but a sadness too. She did not understand, but it was gone even as she saw it, and then, smoothly, confidently, he was turning to his dark-suited companions, leading her forward.

'It's most unfair that a man of my years should hold a young woman's hand and not introduce her to his most important colleagues. When I carry out the introductions, my dear, let me emphasize that the order in which they are made suggests nothing other than convenience.'

The big, slow-moving man laughed as he stepped forward. 'Don't listen to him, Miss Vallance. He's just trying to needle us. I'm Paul Dorset, and I'm happy to meet you.'

His teeth were perfect, his smile broad, but his eyes carried no reflection of the smile. He was more than six feet tall and dwarfed her; his hands were large and should have been clumsy but their touch was surprisingly deft, delicate, his fingertips soft and gentle. He spoke in a slow drawl as he explained he was John Torrance's legal adviser, albeit a company man in boardroom terms, and as Torrance himself eased back, Paul Dorset demonstrated his own brand of charm as he turned Tina to face the second dark-suited executive.

'Miss Vallance . . . Peter Barclay. You could say that Peter sort of looks after the books, so keep your hand on your pocketbook.'

Barclay was dark-eyebrowed and darkhaired. The hair was cut short, *en brosse*, the eyebrows were shaggy, fly-away in shape, beetling in intensity. She guessed he was not a man who would laugh easily and he lacked the capacity to relax as Paul Dorset could in company. But she got the impression that Barclay was trying to learn, with the assiduity of an accountant. He was trying to subdue the aggressiveness of his eyebrows, soften the iron of his mouth, remove the audit from his glance. He smiled, but he could not hide the cold searching of his eyes. She knew he would always remain unconvinced by externals; he would always seek the grime he believed lay behind everything and everyone.

She did not like him and showed it in the quick way she detached herself from his handshake. He was unmoved. Cold in his calculations, he was as alert as a man expecting a knife in his back. She suspected he would have enemies who would one day surprise him. But not yet. Maybe not for a long while.

19

When he stepped back from her, he almost bowed, stiffly. Paul Dorset nodded genially, then turned to glance back towards John Torrance, smiling conspiratorially as though he and Torrance shared a common despair of Barclay's lack of social graces. As Tina caught the glance she wondered whether it would, in the end, be Dorset who would wield the knife Barclay feared.

Torrance did not share the conspiracy of Dorset's smile; he was reaching for his brandy glass again, his eyes hooded, careless of the manoeuvrings undertaken by his henchmen. Dorset touched Tina's elbow, led her forward to meet the third of the younger men in the room.

It was the man who had been standing on the steps of the manor house. He had looked up to her and smiled. It had occasioned an odd resentment in her then, and it did so again now as, before Paul Dorset could speak, the man stuck out his hand. The grip was warm and friendly. Yet its confidence annoyed her.

'I'm Neil Bradon. We've already met.'

In the background Peter Barclay moved, turning slowly to observe them. Paul Dorset, too, was surprised. 'You've already met?'

'More or less. When we were unloading the cars, I saw her standing at the window, watching us.'

'I do *own* Oakham,' Tina said freezingly.

Unabashed, Neil Bradon grinned at her, with a clean, American smile. 'Oh, don't get me wrong. I enjoyed the vision.'

'Vision?' Tina asked, in spite of herself.

'Well, that's right. It was just like one of those old films, you know? Strange, historic, beautiful old house, rooted in ancient traditions and mystery. Arrival of a young, clean-cut hero, standing in the courtyard, bemused. He looks up to the windows and framed there he sees the vision, a half-seen, elfin creature, a whisper from the past, distant, untouchable, separated by the gulf of time, it seems, but then in the last reel—'

'I think I've seen that film,' Tina interrupted cuttingly. 'Isn't it the one where the creature crawls out of the lake, covered in slime, and strangles the clean-cut young man, claiming him for its own?'

Paul Dorset chuckled, a bubbling enjoyment from deep in his throat. 'I like it. She's put you right in your place, Neil.'

But Bradon was not put out of his stride in the least. His eyes were very blue and full of mockery as he stared at Tina. Tina recognized the mockery and was annoyed by it: Bradon would be a young man with a sense of humour and a character and presence that would be pleasing to women. He would be able to mock them, and make them enjoy it. But would he ever be capable of self-mockery? She doubted it. He was too egotistical for that.

'I don't think you saw the end of that film,' he was continuing. 'It was all a put-up job, you see: the hero only *seemed* to be strangled. He was a nice guy, just trying to protect the environment in which the creature existed. And he got the girl in the last reel.'

'Real life is far removed from that kind of synthetic rubbish,' Tina said dismissively, and turned back to John Torrance. 'I thought I should call in to . . . welcome you.'

His eyes were amused; he had caught the slight hesitation. 'That's kind. We'll be as little trouble as we can.'

'There shouldn't be much disturbance, Miss Vallance,' Paul Dorset interposed, moving across to stand beside John Torrance's chair. 'We'll be in conference most of the time; the phones will be pretty busy, and there'll be a few people joining us from time to time, but since you're tucked away in your wing you shouldn't see too much of us.'

'That'll be fine,' Tina said. She was vaguely aware of movement behind her left shoulder; Peter Barclay, edging casually towards John Torrance, to take up station on his left side. 'Will there be some opportunity during these couple of weeks to talk about . . . about the future of the Manor?'

Both men glanced at John Torrance where he sat between them under the protection of their flanking approach. Torrance inspected the brandy in his glass. 'My aides have made their introductions but, like me, have failed to be polite enough to offer you a drink, to join me.'

Barclay was already moving when she shook her head. 'No, thank you. But a little conversation would be welcome.'

The tartness of her reply brought a glint to John Torrance's eyes. He frowned. 'Conversation about our plans? It's a little early for that, Miss Vallance.'

'For you, perhaps. Not for me. I've been waiting for some months for the opportunity to talk to you. I wouldn't want these weeks to go by without getting the chance. And now — before you get down to whatever business you're transacting here — seems like a good time to me.'

His glance was appraising. She had the impression that people rarely spoke to John Torrance so directly. He waved his glass vaguely. 'Well, I apologize for the . . . distance that has been kept between us by my aides. As I said, they tend to be overprotective. But what can I say? No decisions have yet been made.'

'You're aware I'm reluctant to sell Oakham Manor?'

'If it's yours to sell,' Paul Dorset intervened softly. 'And the option is binding, believe me.'

Tina ignored him. She stared at Torrance. 'When will we be able to have a talk, and when will you feel able to make a decision?'

Torrance seemed suddenly tired, though it could hardly be the result of the pressure she was bringing upon him now. He sipped his brandy, and then rose from his chair, glass in hand. 'I'll tell you what my immediate plans are, Miss Vallance, and then we'll take it from there. You've agreed that we can use this house for a couple of weeks, at a price which I believe was more than fair from your point of view.' His mouth hardened at the edges. 'For me, the first week I'm here will be something of a rest. My colleagues here will be setting up various matters in connection with our business. I shall take the chance to get to know Oakham Manor, and see some of your lovely countryside. Then, we all go to Paris.'

'And when you come back?' Tina insisted.

In a cold voice John Torrance said, 'When I come back various decisions of importance will be made. You can include among them our determination of what to do about the option. Now, if you'll excuse me . . .'

He held out his brandy glass, almost empty.

Paul Dorset took it, set it down and Torrance bowed slightly in an old-world manner that contained a hint of stiff mockery, and walked from the room. Tina was not pleased; she felt she had been dismissed. Paul Dorset touched her arm. 'Please, Miss Vallance, don't be upset. He's had a long journey; at his age, it tells.'

Neil Bradon laughed, a short barking, almost impatient sound. 'Tired, hell! Impatient, you mean. John Torrance doesn't get tired—'

'He's seventy, Neil,' Dorset said mildly.

'And a tough old bird who can still see you two out of the window!'

'And you also, Bradon,' Peter Barclay warned. 'Don't ever forget that.'

Bradon was grinning, his clean-cut good looks lit mischievously. 'But I'm not *important* enough to get thrown out. Come on, I'm in a different league, and a different business.'

Paul Dorset was smiling, turning to Tina, smooth, gentle and persuasive. 'I'm sure Miss Vallance is not interested in an exposure of the ragged edges of our business relationships. But can I ask you, Miss Vallance — you made no comment when Mr Torrance spoke about your right to sell Oakham. Can you tell me whether there's been any movement on the matter?'

'Andrew Castle and I are in dispute,' Tina said coolly. 'The issue is being heard, on adjournment, very shortly.'

'And a decision . . . ?'

'You're the lawyer,' she said tartly. 'You tell me. *I'm* hoping that it will be settled within the next two weeks. My solicitors assure me this should be so. But—'

'I know, the law's delays.' Dorset smiled. 'Well, we'll have to wait to see what happens. Either way, we'll be making a decision about the Manor during the second week we're here. You can be pretty confident about that.'

Neil Bradon helped himself to a glass of brandy and winked at Tina. 'What Paul means is that John Torrance will make a decision about the Manor.'

Peter Barclay's mouth twisted as he glared at Bradon, with the glass in his hand. Neither he nor Dorset had taken advantage of Torrance's absence as Bradon had; Tina was left with the feeling that both still felt aware of his presence in the house and the tension prevented them from relaxing. 'Mr Torrance will take the decision on our advice — and he needs our support, rather more than he does yours, Bradon.'

Neil Bradon waved his glass magnanimously. 'Ah, I don't deny it. You're the good guys; I'm the one in the black hat who tells all the lies around the place. Or so I'm told.'

Dorset's tone was genial, but his eyes held hints of annoyance at Bradon's flippancy. 'Neil exaggerates, as usual. I don't know why it is, Miss Vallance, but advertising men always tend to take a rather different view of the world from straightforward businessmen like ourselves.'

'*Straightforward*!' Bradon spluttered over his brandy, and grinned at Tina, shaking his head. There was something infectious about the grin; she armoured her own mouth against it. 'Well, I hope you'll find all you need—'

'Before you go, Miss Vallance, it might be useful if you could give me a rundown on the general situation with regard to Oakham Manor.' Peter Barclay was stepping forward, his shaggy eyebrows beetling thoughtfully. 'I gather it includes two farms—'

'They aren't paying propositions,' Tina said.

'And the acreage—'

'Is smaller than you might have been led to believe by Mr Castle.'

'I assure you—'

'Oh, come *on*, Mr Barclay.' Tina was suddenly aware of Neil Bradon's grin again and angrily she went on, 'Don't try to tell me you've had no discussions with Andrew Castle!

He's never lived here so doesn't have the total picture, but he is a *possible* owner, and I can hardly believe you wouldn't have had some discussions with him about Oakham Manor!'

Barclay's dark eyes were stony. 'Mr Castle does not have access to the books of account for the estate. Not yet.'

'Or ever!' she flashed.

'That remains to be seen,' Barclay said obstinately, as Paul Dorset swayed unhappily in the background, wanting to smooth over a possible disturbance. 'But I will need to have access to the accounts before I can offer appropriate advice to Mr Torrance.'

'Why should I show you the accounts? I don't even want to sell Oakham Manor!'

Barclay was unmoved. 'On the assumption you have the *right* to sell the Manor, you will need to let me have sight of the financial situation. The option we hold—'

'To hell with the option!'

Barclay's cold eyes glittered. He leaned forward, predatorily. 'It's a mistake to allow emotion to interfere with business, Miss Vallance. It seems to me you need a lesson—'

'Now hold on.' Paul Dorset was moving forward, imposing his heavy bulk between Tina and the menacing accountant. 'I don't think we need take this matter of the option any further at this stage. It's all a bit early. The books can wait. Everything can wait, until we all get to know each other a bit better, until legal issues are resolved, and until John Torrance gets the . . . feel of the place.'

'And then there's my advice, as well,' Neil Bradon interposed cheerfully. 'It's not to be discounted, you know!'

Dorset ignored him. 'In the meanwhile, we'll try to make sure we don't get in your way too much, Miss Vallance. And in a couple of weeks, maybe to our mutual satisfaction, things will be . . . resolved.'

The last words had a curious effect on all three men. Neil Bradon smiled again, somewhat contemptuously, as he looked at Dorset. Something happened to Peter Barclay's face: the line of his jaw tightened and he seemed to draw down shutters, retreat behind curtains of impassivity, damping down his irritation with Tina Vallance in the face of fires of greater moment. As for Dorset himself, he blinked in vague, momentary surprise — as though the words had crept out unbidden and he had been caught unawares by the naked wantonness of the phrase. There was a short silence. Then Neil Bradon snorted.

'You're not going to tell her then?'

Dorset's normal urbanity had almost returned; now he glared angrily at Bradon. 'I don't think—'

'Tell me what?' Tina demanded.

Dorset hesitated, flashed one more angry glance in Bradon's direction, and then turned to Tina. 'This . . . er . . . dispute you have with Mr Castle over the ownership of Oakham Manor, I trust there's no *personal* animosity involved?'

'Personal animosity? What the hell are you talking about? Castle wants me out of here and I can't say I'm too pleased about it!'

Dorset's eyes were as cold as Barclay's now as he made his calculations, searching her face. 'We were talking a little while ago about the books and you suggested we would have been in touch with Mr Castle. The fact is, we have. And we've invited him down here to the Manor.'

'The hell you have!'

'We deemed it necessary that he should join us for a few days, for discussions concerning the future of the Manor.'

'He doesn't own Oakham! He's no right to come here!'

'I'm sorry you object—'

'I *certainly* object!'

Dorset's mouth was rigid. After a moment he said, 'I *am* sorry you object, but matters have been arranged. Since, as I understand it, we have the use of the Manor for a period, the matter of whom we invite to join us during our tenure is entirely within our discretion. I agree it might seem a little unfortunate—'

'Crass, even,' Neil Bradon murmured happily.

'Unfortunate, but nevertheless necessary. We shall naturally take your objection into account and ensure that as little embarrassment as possible is caused to you.'

Tina clenched her fists in frustration. Contemptuously she said, 'Is there anything else?'

Barclay stepped forward. 'The staff you've retained on our behalf. We'll need one or two more people apart from our own. I presume there's an agency of some kind we can contact . . .'

Tina gave him the name of an agency. There was a short silence. The three men stood staring at her but something had changed in the atmosphere: there was a tension in the room she was unable to explain. Since John Torrance had left, the cement that bound these three men together in the semblance of a working system seemed to have disappeared. But that was their problem, not hers, and abruptly she turned on her heel and walked towards the door.

As she looked back, closing the door, she saw that both Dorset and Barclay had turned away; only Neil Bradon was still watching her. He had not dismissed her like the others, but his glance was thoughtful and enigmatic: it seemed out of place with his general air of cheerful flippancy.

Tina returned to her room. She did not like these men, any of them: the book-balancing accountant, the smooth lawyer, the chameleon advertising executive. And John Torrance . . . he was an old man, tough, strong and experienced. He was bringing Andrew McNeil Castle to *her* house, to run his greedy eyes over the inheritance he claimed. She clearly ranked small in John Torrance's scheme of things, as did the matter of her feelings. And none of them would ever care the way she did about Oakham Manor, about life here, about what would be destroyed if they took it over, for whatever purposes they really wished to acquire it.

To them, she and it were both so small, so unimportant.

If she cried now they would not see the tears. It seemed important to her, nevertheless, that she should *not* cry, not even now in the privacy of her own rooms. Time yet for tears, when all was lost beyond redemption.

4

It was cool in the old kitchens. They had long ago ceased to be used for their original purposes: more modern arrangements had been established above. Now the stone-flagged floor was empty, its grey, scored surface dusty in the afternoon sun that streamed in from the tall windows along the outside wall, with only the massive stone fireplaces and chimneys to stand beside the ovens as evidence of the room's reason for existence.

Arnold had come down again to sit, and think. He had worked all morning in the library as he had done each morning since the arrival of the American contingent. He understood they would be leaving next day but it made little difference to him for he had seen little of them. One, a young man called Neil Bradon, had spent a certain amount of time with him in the library, questioning his activity in a direct, ingenuous way. Arnold had liked him: there was a brashness that overlay Bradon's manner but it was a superficial veneer that Arnold suspected had been placed there for a purpose. Underneath there was a more sensitive individual than the surface suggested. Even businessmen could be human, Arnold admitted. Though perhaps not many of them.

Things had certainly changed once the American contingent had taken up residence. The entourage had bustled around in the way all businessmen bustled, seemingly busy but probably not. Energy could bring results, and activity more, but Arnold also believed that pure cerebration could achieve just as much. That was what Arnold had been doing when Andrew McNeil Castle had walked into the library: just cerebrating.

'Quiet place to get your head down,' Castle said, with a snort.

'I wasn't asleep. I was thinking,' Arnold had replied.

'My old mother used to go out like a light, regular, seven every evening. Snored like a hog. Wake her, she'd deny it. Restin' my eyes, she used to say. Restin' my eyes, thassall.'

Arnold had not liked Andrew McNeil Castle. To be fair, Arnold was no doubt influenced by the reaction of Tina Vallance to Castle's presence at Oakham Manor: he liked the girl and felt sorry for her, and could understand how she felt about the presence of Andrew Castle in her home when they were in litigation about its ownership. But, equally, he resented the possessive air with which Castle had inspected the library.

'Worth much, all this stuff?'

Arnold stared coolly at the man. He was only about five feet six inches tall but his lack of inches was exaggerated by his girth. He wore slacks and a loose, short-sleeved shirt which did little to hide his spreading belly, and his hands were stubby, red hair sprouting on their knuckles. He was almost bald, with just a few stubborn tufts of red-grey hair above his ears and his face had a lived-in look about it, the flesh sagging around his mouth and neck, his eyes deeply pouched, his lips petulant.

'Value can be measured in different ways,' Arnold replied. 'If you mean could you get much money for these papers, well, I guess a museum would pay a reasonable sum for some of the older materials. But it wouldn't amount to much.'

'Not even as a collection?'

'The papers have an intrinsic historical value, but I hardly think they'd be worth selling.'

29

Castle appeared to lose interest in the papers at that stage and had moved around the library, strutting with his hands behind his back and viewing the shelves as though he already owned them. Arnold was glad when the accountant called Barclay arrived, to call Castle to conference with himself and Paul Dorset. Barclay affected to ignore Arnold, but that suited Arnold very well. He did not like the man's cold eyes.

But he had not come down here to the kitchens to think about Andrew McNeil Castle, or the crassness of the Torrance contingent in bringing Castle to Oakham Manor when Tina would clearly be upset by his presence. He had seen Castle leave, after a curiously conspiratorial discussion with Paul Dorset at his car, and now the man was gone he should be dismissed from his mind. Arnold was down here because he was tired of working in the library, and at the back of his mind there lay a problem, a puzzle that had been bothering him. Peace of mind would not come until he had solved that puzzle. So he leaned against the wall for a while, sat on one of the broken pendants for a half hour or so and stared and thought and reasoned.

And waited.

Patience could bring solutions.

But not on this occasion. Sighing, he rose to his feet at last and brushed down his trousers to remove the dust of years. He walked across the kitchen area towards the stairs. They led out into the courtyard. The heavy oaken door — sixteenth-century, he calculated — had been one of the first things he had attended to. Disused for many years, it had required oiling along the hinges, and he had undertaken the job several days previously. Now it moved easily, almost soundlessly. He pushed at it, and smiled as it moved as smoothly as on the day it had been hung.

There was a man standing in the courtyard, staring upwards, and he had not heard the door opening, so remained unaware of Arnold's presence.

He was not tall; he stood staring about him, elderly and curiously defenceless as though he felt dwarfed by the massive stone walls that surrounded him in the courtyard, humbled by the expanse of blue sky above. It was as though he stood there seeking something, and was uneasy as he searched. Arnold knew who it was, although they had not formally met, and he had indeed seen him at the Manor, but never like this, alone, with his defences down, a small, lonely, perhaps tired old man suddenly uncertain of what he was or why. Arnold felt he was intruding upon a private moment and he hesitated, not certain whether he should try to cross the courtyard or wait until the man moved away. Yet if he stayed as he was, it was as though he were spying. He stepped forward; the sound of his movement drew the other man out of his reverie. He turned, stared at Arnold, and he shed his vulnerability like a skin.

'Hi!'

'Hello.' Arnold nodded, then added feebly, 'It's a nice day.'

'Right. You . . . you're the guy who's working up in the library?' When Arnold agreed, the man with the iron-grey hair came forward and shook hands. 'I'm John Torrance.'

'Arnold Landon. I . . . I've been taking a rest from the library to look around the manor house.'

'I understand. I came out too. Been admiring the architecture,' Torrance lied. 'They certainly built these places to last!'

Embarrassed by his knowledge of moments ago, Arnold said, 'Not really.'

John Torrance stared at him. 'England's full of splendid mediaeval buildings! All the guidebooks say so, and everyone knows how splendidly they built in the old days!'

Arnold shrugged, looked around him at the stout walls of the courtyard. 'Don't be fooled, Mr Torrance. Mediaeval architecture was ephemeral.'

John Torrance smiled; it was a charming smile, calculated to draw a man. 'What's that supposed to mean?'

'You say how splendidly they built — the old monks who started Oakham Manor. But here, and in the churches and cathedrals, we only see what *survived*.'

'So—'

'What about all the other buildings they must have erected?' Arnold waved his hand around him, gesturing towards the solid granite walls. 'We only see what survived, and the survival is due to an unscientific and uneconomic prodigality of building materials. In the fifteenth century there were still, certainly, master masons who combined tradition, experience and genius — but they were rare. What we see of fifteenth-century building now is nothing more than the results of prodigality and the mellowing accidents of time.'

John Torrance folded his arms and gazed at Arnold. His head came forward, as though to peer more closely at this unusual specimen. Arnold shuffled under the scrutiny. 'I'm sorry. I shouldn't—'

'No, hold on, Mr Landon,' John Torrance interrupted. 'It's more fun listening to firmly held views than to half-baked theories from guidebooks. You've made a study of architecture?'

'Not exactly. It's part of my interest—'

'So tell me more. Prodigality, you said . . . and time. At my age I'm interested in both.'

Arnold shrugged. 'Well, if you look into the records, you'll find that nothing was more common than to find that churches built in, say, the eleventh century, fell down soon after they were built, or certainly within fifty years.'

'Is that so?'

'That's so,' Arnold repeated gravely. 'Of the great Norman towers a considerable proportion collapsed sooner rather than later. Evesham went in nine-sixty, Ramsey Abbey in nine-eighty-five. Abingdon is further testimony: that fell in ten-ninety-one. A gale in the same year unroofed St Mary at Bow and reduced other churches to ruin. It's true that the wind lifted twenty-six-foot beams and drove them twenty feet into the ground, but that was unusual. You can look at Dunstable in twelve-ten, Bury St Edmunds, two towers at Chichester and Master Thomas de Northwich's tower at Evesham.'

He paused, aware that once he was launched he could become the biggest bore in the north of England. John Torrance lifted an eyebrow. 'There could be an explanation.'

'What?'

'Maybe England in the twelfth century was a hurricane epicentre.'

Arnold regarded him seriously. 'When in eleven-seven the central tower at Winchester fell, the reason was said to be the wickedness of William Rufus.'

'And you think . . . ?' Torrance twinkled at him.

'I think — not unreasonably — it was due to defective foundations.'

Both men laughed, and there was a warmth growing between them. They walked slowly together around the courtyard in the afternoon sun, and Torrance listened as Arnold talked. He was a receptive listener, interjecting occasional questions but in the main prepared to let Arnold ramble, explain, delineate a society of workmen long since gone.

Arnold told him about the great buildings that had gone and about the men who had built them. He told him about the mediaeval architects who had been combinations of master mason, carpenter, draughtsman, not above copying or drawing inspiration from the work of others. 'They were site managers too, and capable of laying their hands on axe and chisel, stone and beam. They'd been apprentices, became masons, master masons, architects. They knew everything because they'd *done* everything. The only thing they really lacked was a scientific training — and the abstract knowledge of stress.'

'Which is why their houses fell down,' Torrance murmured. 'Things haven't changed much, have they?'

'How do you mean?' Arnold asked.

'Those men, the architects five hundred years ago, they'd worked their way up but they lacked . . . what did you say? Scientific training and the abstract knowledge of stress. It can be like that in business. You work your way up, you develop, but it's by experience, the seat of your pants, gut feelings.

33

Not training. And things can go wrong . . . not least in the men you employ.'

Arnold agreed. He talked about the other problems faced by the master masons. He told Torrance about the guilds. He explained how the Oxford Guilds had interfered with the outside workmen, the people who were not members, and caused them to stay away under the pressure. He explained how the carpenters and slaters in Oxford could claim only two members each — but still formed themselves into guilds to enforce restrictive practices: till the better of the two carpenters completely spoiled one house and made another's roof two feet shorter than the walls. 'Cromwell summed it up, you know, when he said: "How proud and false the workmen be!"'

John Torrance raised a quizzical eyebrow. 'So criticisms of modern workmanship . . . ?'

Arnold shook his head. 'Ah, let's be clear about it; bad workmanship is not the monopoly of our own generation. The mediaeval craftsman-architect could create masterpieces, but he could also make as bad blunders as any of his glass-walled-office successors in modern times. And as to the workmen — if the British workman is not as good as he used to be, well, my answer is he probably never was!'

Torrance laughed loudly. Arnold suspected it was a reaction rare in the businessman. Torrance glanced at him obliquely and nodded. 'I've enjoyed our conversation, Mr Landon. There are things to think upon; things yet to learn. I think we should talk again. You work in the library . . . but why are you down here?'

Arnold glanced back towards the kitchens. 'There's something that puzzles me.'

'In there?'

Arnold nodded. 'And elsewhere. It's about something I found in the library, regarding the construction of Oakham Manor.'

'Interesting. You must tell me about it.' Torrance consulted his watch, and hesitated. 'But not now; I have a meeting. Tomorrow?'

'It would be my pleasure,' Arnold said, glowing. 'But I thought you were leaving in the morning.'

'For Paris.' Torrance smiled. 'But if I can't, at my age, order my existence, who can? Till tomorrow, Mr Landon.'

As he walked away, the old man had a jauntiness about his step that suggested the uncertainties of an hour ago were forgotten.

* * *

That evening, at the inn where the Heritage Society had arranged accommodation for Arnold, he mused over the conversation he had had with John Torrance. There had been some kind of spark kindled between them; he liked the old man. Perhaps it was the result of Torrance's almost innocent interest in what he had been talking about: a good listener always endeared himself to the speaker. And yet there was more to it than that. Arnold had received the impression that John Torrance was *learning* from him. He had no idea what it was that he could teach the businessman; their worlds were so far apart, the head of a large American company could have little in common with a planning officer who lacked academic and professional qualifications and whose only claim to fame was a deep interest in men and materials of the past. He suspected it might have been merely the mood of the moment; an hour in a busy life, a change, a rest, a relief from pressure to listen to a stream of inconsequentialities. It would be an explanation. Morning would bring back a sense of values and of time. There would be no postponement of the Paris arrangements. There would be no further discussions regarding the history of Oakham Manor.

The steak was good; the glass of Médoc satisfying. The evening was long. For a little while, as he faced realities, Arnold Landon felt lonely.

* * *

When John Torrance entered the library the following morning Arnold was surprised, and more than a little flustered. 'I'm flattered,' he said.

'That I should want to spend some time with you?' Torrance shrugged; he was dressed in a dark-grey sweater and slacks that emphasized the leanness of his body and made him seem younger than his seventy years. 'You shouldn't be. It's a pleasure for me to escape the . . . problems that surround me, and I welcome the chance to *listen* for a while. Besides, some of the things you talked to me about yesterday, well, I guess they've been on my mind a bit.'

'I don't understand.'

'Nor do I, not too much. But you've reawakened in me a sense of history, you know what I mean? It sort of helps put things in perspective.'

'I can understand the feeling, but its application in your case—'

'Well, never mind. My problems are my problems. Except, what you said about mediaeval workmen, and the guilds, and the way in which time sort of distances our view of things, so we don't see the reality, not even in stone . . . It sort of got to me . . .'

Arnold smiled. 'Ah well, that's something we all have to come to terms with at some time or another. I tell you, I came across a book here in the library the other day . . . something I read long ago. Forrest . . . *The History of Grisild the Second*—' He hunted briefly along the shelves until he located the leather-bound volume, its gilt faded, its edges scuffed and marked. 'Here it is. There's a passage in it, here it is . . . it sort of brings home to you the fact that nothing changes, you know?'

He waited while John Torrance read the passage; the businessman skimmed it, read it a second time, then looked up. 'Never come across this before. Interesting . . . may I borrow it for a while?'

Arnold hesitated. 'It belongs here in the library. It would be for Miss Vallance to say . . .'

'Of course,' Torrance said smoothly. 'And I imagine the volume is fairly valuable.' He handed the book back, but not before glancing at its title once more. 'Anyway, you were going to tell me about Oakham Manor and its puzzles.'

'I was a bit carried away—'

'No, please, tell me,' Torrance insisted. 'I've put off my Paris trip because I was interested — and I *do* have an option on the place after all!'

Arnold hesitated, then walked across to the far end of the table on which he was working, to forage among a pile of papers that he had stacked at the corner. He checked through them for a while, then extracted a sheet of notes. 'I've been cataloguing various things here, and some of the documents are quite old. In fact, they shouldn't be held here at all — County Archives would be a better place, even if very few people got to see them at all. Some of the older stuff concerns the provenance of Oakham Manor; they are copies of original documents dating back to the fifteenth century. One of them relates to the building of the tower.'

John Torrance raised his eyebrows. 'Oakham doesn't have a tower that I've seen.'

'It fell down fifty years after completion,' Arnold said and they both laughed.

'What else?'

Arnold checked his sheet of notes. 'Well, there's this, which I find intriguing. There's a series of ancient building contracts, relating to the construction of the house. They're unique, of course, and quite valuable. A number of such contracts are held in the Bodleian and elsewhere, but new finds of this kind are always of interest. There's one which tells of the building of part of Oakham. The mason was a man called Waiter; he was under the instructions of the abbot. You'll recall the building started out as an abbey.'

'So you told me.'

'Waiter, it seems, was a poor glassworker before he took over the task, so what *his* history was would be a fascinating study! Anyway, this was the bit that really puzzled me. Just a

passage. It says that, and I paraphrase from the original Latin —
arranging in it many hiding-places and passages fit to accomplish his design
. . . that's what it says. In the original Latin, *latebras et diverticula*,
hiding-places and passages. And fit to accomplish his design? It
just makes me wonder — what design, what purpose?'

'Religious persecution?' John Torrance suggested, with
a shrug.

'Possibly. But not at that time. I suppose it's just one
of those things, little puzzles that bother you in the night,
problems that beset you.'

'I have a few of my own,' John Torrance remarked drily.
'This was the reason for your visit down below yesterday?'

'To the old kitchens?' Arnold shook his head. 'No, not
really. That was something else.' He laughed ruefully. 'I
should really spend my time and energy and thought here in
the library, but so many other things interest me about the
Manor that I have to keep sneaking off to wander around,
working things out.'

John Torrance grinned, like a schoolboy stealing a treat.
'I have the same feeling right now. So what is it with the old
kitchens?'

Arnold stood up. 'I'll show you.'

He led the way from the library, crossing the broad
panelled landing and down the curving staircase that led to
the courtyard. At the doorway, he saw a young man standing, his back to the light. It was Neil Bradon, tall, massive
against the brightness. He ignored Arnold, and spoke directly
to his employer. 'Mr Torrance? I understand the Paris flight
is postponed.'

'We're leaving tomorrow morning instead, Neil. Didn't
Paul tell you? An old man's whim.'

'The press—'

'Tomorrow, Neil.' Torrance cut him short and brushed
past. As he walked beside Arnold across the courtyard, he
whispered mischievously, 'You've caused quite a turmoil in
the Torrance camp, Mr Landon. But I'm enjoying it. It's
time I took the opportunity to learn . . . and think.'

Arnold glanced uncertainly at his companion. For the first time he began to question Torrance's actions. It seemed irrational for the head of a large American company to drop, suddenly, his business plans merely to keep company with a man like Arnold Landon. And these comments about *learning*? Still, it was Torrance's business . . . and Arnold, too, enjoyed the opportunity to indulge his own interests, and talk about them to someone who was prepared to listen. So few people were prepared to listen.

So he talked to John Torrance in the kitchens.

'You see, these days there's an excessive preoccupation with surviving mediaeval stonework. It's a failure to grasp the realities of mediaeval life that brings about that kind of preoccupation. Builders did not work primarily in stone, but in wood. The vast majority of buildings weren't castles and churches . . . they were humble earth and wattle dwellings, and wood was the common material. And I should tell you, wood has been my life's passion; its warmth, its texture, its strength, its properties, its agelessness, its beauty. They knew about those things in the old days, and especially its beauty . . . Until the eleventh century even churches were built of wood. Lindisfarne was built of cleft oak, you know, and the castles in Stephen's anarchical reign were made of wood, too. All right, maybe they were really more like timber-crowned mounds than castles, but even so . . .'

And as they stood in the quiet, cool stone kitchens of Oakham Manor Arnold told him all about the past, and about his father and his carpenter's love of wood, about his own research, his own knowledge, his own feeling for the ancient materials. He explained how the timber-constructed roof was to be regarded as perhaps the most notable feature of English architecture, for stone roofs were far less common in old England than they had been on the continent. He described how pairs of rafters spanned the roofs with their feet pegged to wall plates. He showed John Torrance, by sketches in the dust, how the rafters were pegged with horizontal beams a third of the length from the ridge, to ensure a rigid stability. He explained about collars and wind-beams, orbyngs and tie-beams . . . and then he told John Torrance what was puzzling him.

'You see, the pressure builds up on the wall plates with such constructions as you see in this roof, above the kitchens. That pressure is counteracted by massive tie-beams.'

'Those'll be the tie-beams, running from one wall plate to the other?'

'That's right,' Arnold said. 'Beams of that kind hold the walls together well enough, but their weight and their size give them a tendency to sag, so additional support has to be provided.'

'Posts?'

'Pillars, sometimes wooden, more often stone . . . at the very least, resting on stone corbels, with a brace morticed into the lower end of the post and the under surface of the tie-beam. The posts were called pendants.'

John Torrance raised his grey head and looked around him, faintly puzzled. 'If you're talking about these kitchens, there aren't any . . . *pendants*, you called them?'

'Oh, please, the roofing structure was changed maybe two hundred years ago. But that doesn't mean the old evidence was destroyed. There *were* pendants in these kitchens, supporting the roof. Here, look, I'll show you . . .'

Torrance followed close behind as Arnold paced out the length of the kitchens carefully. When he knelt, Torrance stood leaning over him.

'You see?' Arnold said softly. 'It's all that remains . . . a raised irregularity, circular in shape, on the flagstones. Removed long ago . . . but there was a stud post here, raised as a pillar with base and capital, set in the centre of the tie-beam up there, and then attached by braces around about there, to the ridge-pieces, and the principals . . . The stud post,' Arnold added inconsequentially, 'was also called, sometimes, a mountant.'

John Torrance stood bemused. He shook his head. 'These traces, they're interesting, though it would need a trained eye to find them. But what I don't understand: what's the puzzle?'

'There's two of them,' Arnold explained simply. 'But they're in the wrong place.'

* * *

It was, he explained as the morning grew late, all a matter of stresses and balances and weight. The old master masons might have had no scientific training, but they learned by trial and error — and passed their knowledge on. When they didn't know, or didn't apply what they had learned, towers and roofs and whole churches fell down. But Oakham Manor had not collapsed and was still standing in modern times. Arnold, however, had an advantage over many of the ancient masons; he had studied the successful work first-hand, and he knew where the stresses of the roofs would be supported.

The problem was, in the kitchens of Oakham Manor, the pendants had not been placed in the positions where they would most efficiently have supported the roof.

'A mistake?'

'I think not. These pendants supported the roof all right, but they're wrongly placed and that needed a third mount-ant. It's over here.'

'So they made a mistake, and this was a failsafe system—'

'I explained to you, Mr Torrance. The oldest buildings remain these days because of a prodigality of materials. They were built uneconomically, with too much being used in way of materials to justify their building at the time. But it's why they've lasted. But this abbey cum manor house . . . While it might have had care and expenditure lavished on it, well, it *still* doesn't make sense that they should defy structural logic *deliberately*.'

'How do you know it was deliberate?'

'Because of the third, normally unnecessary, pendant. It all meant *money*, Mr Torrance. And people don't throw money away, in any age. It puzzles me.'

John Torrance was silent for a while. He appeared to be deep in thought. At last he said quietly, 'You've been thinking about this for some days, Mr Landon.'

'Yes.'

'And with no result. I wonder . . . outsiders . . . they have a way of looking at things from a different angle. Different from the viewpoint of the person who *knows* what he's about, or thinks he does. I have a feeling you've done that for me, in one sense, in *my* problems. Maybe I can return the compliment.'

'I don't understand.'

'You've got another puzzle on your mind, haven't you? The document? *Latebras et diverticula*?'

For several seconds Arnold stared at John Torrance while his mind flicked over the romantic impossibilities. He shook his head, as much as anything to quell the growing excitement in his chest. He turned, walked silently across the kitchen. Methodically he paced, measuring, calculating. After a while he explained to the silent businessman what he was trying to do; when Torrance also started pacing the task was halved.

When the hollow ringing of the flagstones changed at last in tone and volume they stared at each other, grinning. They paced again, striking the flagstones and the walls and time slipped by until, in the late afternoon, when hunger was gnawing away at their excitement, Arnold finally discovered the pillar, and the crumbling cement, and the entrance. John Torrance hurried away to get a torch.

He returned fifteen minutes later, grumbling. 'You run a company worth a million dollars and your aides can't find you a torch! Barclay finally got one for me from one of the cars.'

Arnold had been waiting just inside the darkness of the entrance. Together the men now explored, the torch beam dancing against the wall of the tunnel. When breathing became difficult they re-emerged, dusty but triumphant and excited. They re-sealed the entrance. They agreed, solemnly, that neither would tell anyone of the entrance to the tunnel until Torrance had had time to return from Paris and they could investigate further, together. This was to be their personal secret. They knew they were behaving like children, like overgrown schoolboys, but they enjoyed the feeling. It came but rarely to a man of seventy and another of fifty.

Arnold left John Torrance in the courtyard and made his way back to the library. He stood at the library window looking down to the courtyard and some of the euphoria drained from him. There was someone down there, walking under the overhang of the roof; Arnold could not see who it was, and wondered whether it was Torrance. There had been no one else to be seen down there, when he and Torrance had emerged from the kitchens.

But there was something else fluttering at the back of Arnold's mind. When he had been alone in the tunnel entrance, waiting for Torrance to bring the torch, the sounds had come: the eerie, whispering, scratching sounds.

Inexplicably, Arnold had told Torrance nothing about them.

CHAPTER TWO

1

It had none of the prestige of the larger courtrooms and none of their excitement or sense of drama. There were just fifteen people sitting behind Tina, and three of them had entered the courtroom, clearly, to find a warm place in which to sleep. In front of her sat the three counsel engaged to dispute the issues: her own man, James Markham, QC, was about to rise to make his closing remarks to the seventy-year-old judge on the Bench, while the two counsel employed by Andrew Castle leaned back in their seats, one openly yawning.

It meant a great deal to her, and, she admitted with reluctance, perhaps to Andrew Castle too, but it drew little by way of fire from Bar, Bench or public. And as Markham began his closing remarks, the gentle hint of his Irish brogue induced a sleepiness in a courtroom already inclined to nod off. She listened as he went over the whole centuries-old story yet again, reminding Mr Justice Quaver of the facts and the issues in dispute.

'Had the Manor of Oakham not changed from its original function as an abbey,' Markham was saying, 'this dispute would never have arisen, but its sale to the Wolfards in the fifteenth century, and the consequent rebuilding that was to

create the fine house that still stands, has led, through tortu-
ous family histories to our present difficulties . . .'

Difficulties. Tina snorted mentally and glanced across
the panelled room to Andrew McNeil Castle. She described
him as her uncle and thought of him as such, but that was
because it was easier than attempting to unravel the precise
relationship — second cousin, twice removed? It made no
difference; he was the adventurer who was seeking to take
Oakham Manor away from her. He did not look like an
adventurer — he was short, stocky, pot-bellied and almost
sixty years of age, with a sagging face and a woman's mouth.
His suits were expensive but ill fitting, and he cut no dash.
Even so, he wanted Oakham as a nest egg with which he
could retire to the States, and the interest displayed in the
Manor by the American company was the chocolate upon
that particular egg.

'. . . but, as was common during the pre-Victorian
period,' Markham was continuing, 'the conveyances to separate branches of the original family included provisos that the
name of Wolfard should be taken by the new incumbent. So
it is that in 1800 and again in 1815 — when, incidentally,
the fortunes of the estate were at a low ebb as a result of the
Napoleonic Wars — the name of Wolfard-Heard appears, each
cousin succeeding his childless relative and adding the name of
Wolfard to his own. The death of Charles Wolfard-Heard in
1825 boded ill for the custom, however; thereafter, as a new line
of the Heard family took possession the name of Wolfard was
taken only twice; by 1880 it emerged no more . . .'

Trees, and lines and successions: a sense of history, a
feeling of family, and yet they said nothing of people's weaknesses, and foibles, and sorrows and loves. Tina had ploughed
her way through papers in the library and struggled through
to her own understanding of what those ancient conveyances
actually described, but it was only in the soft darkness of her
own room at Oakham, on misty early mornings, that she
could look out of the window and begin to know her ances-
tors, those distant, different people who had walked across

those fields, planted those trees, and perhaps felt the sense of pride and *belonging* that she did. Andrew McNeil Castle could know nothing of that any more than CADS could ever begin to understand.

'. . . so, in essence, we are faced with two contentions. The line from which my client traces her descent is without doubt that which comes from *Thomas* Wolfard, who died in fourteen-twenty-four. He had a posthumous son, but too late; the ownership of Oakham had passed to Thomas's brother *William* Wolfard. The first contention of my client is, therefore, that in law that succession is insupportable: the estates should legitimately have gone to the son of Thomas Wolfard and, consequently, directly to my client in due time.' The barrister paused, shuffling his papers in front of him. 'And the second contention is that Andrew McNeil Castle, who claims descent from the body of William Wolfard, has failed to prove his case on the balance of probabilities. The provenance of his claim arises out of family papers in the United States; parish records in Norfolk, Devon and Norwich; two conveyances descriptive of his family tree, and — what else? Nothing of substance, and in any case a break in 1833 which must cause great doubts to arise regarding the validity of his claim. Thus, our contention is, even if the court *should* rule, against our argument, that the conveyance of Oakham Manor to William Wolfard in fourteen-twenty-four was legal, we would still wish consideration of the claim of Andrew McNeil Castle as spurious, not soundly rooted in evidence, and of doubtful, seriously doubtful provenance . . .'

Mr Justice Quaver seemed unimpressed, but then, Tina thought, the lugubrious set of his features had displayed little emotion of any kind during the hearings, other than resigned boredom. Yet in his hands lay the future of Oakham Manor. Markham had sat down; Quaver was saying something she could not follow. Markham rose as the judge did, and the whole court rose with them. When Mr Justice Quaver had hobbled out, Markham turned to Tina and gave her a tight, professional smile. 'He's reserved judgment.'

'What does that mean?'

Markham gathered his papers together and glanced at his watch. 'He'll be giving a written opinion, in a few days, or a couple of weeks. He's always a bit slow on these things — likes to weigh up the pros and cons. Nothing hasty. But I must dash — due in Queen's Bench in five minutes. We'll be in touch.'

Tina watched him as he swept out. There was something of the impatient waitress about the legal profession: they always seemed to want to move on to the next table. Throw down the menu and run.

Tina made her way out into the Strand. Rain streamed down from a cold grey sky and she raised the collar of her raincoat, cursing the fact that she had brought no umbrella. She hesitated, walked to the edge of the pavement and a taxi drove past, sending up a bow wave that drenched her legs and inflamed her mood. The glare that she would have sent after the taxi-driver was directed elsewhere as she heard the voice behind her.

'If you stay there too long, you'll need to learn to swim!'

She hated his clean-cut good looks and his confident, assertive manner. She decided to ignore both.

'You can probably use this, Miss Vallance.'

She hated his black, massively protective umbrella too, but she needed it and as he took a grip on her elbow, steered her into the gap in the traffic and towed her across the street she was angrily grateful for its succour.

'Where are you headed?'

'For something to drink.'

'There's a tea shop—'

'Whisky,' Tina said balefully.

Neil Bradon smiled. His teeth were even and regular as all American teeth were, his eyes friendly, his grin infectious and he even seemed *dry* under the umbrella. 'I thought young English ladies were tea-addicted.'

'Not when they've just been through an experience in a court of law,' Tina grumbled, and scurried for the Wig and Pen. Neil Bradon followed her, elaborately shaking the umbrella and refolding it. She stood inside the doorway of the pub, steaming slightly, her hair plastered to her head, water trickling down her face, and annoyed that the exigencies of the moment had allowed her to accept the presence of this objectionable young American.

'Whisky?' he checked before shouldering his way to the bar, through conversation and damp suits. When he returned she had found a seat in the corner, behind the door, and he squeezed in beside her. She eyed the umbrella sourly. 'I thought Americans laughed at Englishmen, about umbrellas.'

'Native populations always know best, climatically speaking.'

'But in no other respect?'

He eyed her carefully. 'There are always . . . improvements that can be made.'

She thought of what they could do to Oakham Manor. 'Not always,' she insisted. 'There are some things that can never be improved, things like a way of life.'

He was on dangerous ground, and he knew it. He glanced around him, smiling slightly. 'Makes a change from Paris.'

'I was surprised to see you a moment ago, in the Strand.'

'Ah well, when we left five or six days ago we all went to Paris—'

'The cavalcade . . .' she murmured.

'—but while John Torrance and the Apostles stayed on I—'

'The *Apostles*?'

He grinned at her with that objectionably open frank grin. 'Don't you see them like that? I've been working for John Torrance for five years now and it struck me as soon as I arrived that the way they cling to him, hang on his words, move close, protectively to him, follow his guiding light and proclaim his everlasting truths, well, it's the only way to describe them. As to which of them will turn out to be the Judas, that's another matter.'

'Is one likely to?'

His glance locked with hers, and suddenly elements of inscrutability had entered those friendly eyes. She realized that behind the surface charm, Neil Bradon was as tough as any of the CADS people she had met. 'In the world of business,' he said softly, 'there's always the possibility of a Judas.'

'And you're as capable of being one as any?' The grin came back, swiftly, as though Neil Bradon realized he had over-exposed himself; honesty retreated behind charm. 'Me, no, I'm just a straightforward Madison Avenue man, out to present the best image possible for the company that employs me.'

'Just an advertising man,' Tina said with a hint of contempt, and sipped her whisky.

'Oh, don't knock it. It's done well enough by me. I worked my way through college — Midwest University — and I came to the Big Apple full of ideas and ambitions. They got knocked out of me within two years, but Madison Avenue gave me my chance, I found my forte, and my foothold on the steep slope that leads—'

'To the top. You even *sound* like an advertising man, talking in clichés.'

He regarded her soberly. After a short silence he said, 'Shall we . . . er . . . start again?'

Tina stared at the golden liquid in her glass.

She knew she was being unpleasant and curt, but there was something about this young American that disturbed her, and she did not like him. Normally, dislike of a person didn't cause her to be rude, but somehow, with Neil Bradon . . . 'I don't think there's any need to start again. I'll have to go in a moment.'

'I was offering an olive branch . . . suggesting a truce.'

'There you go, clichés again.'

He laughed. 'Just what the hell *is* it with you?'

She finished her whisky with great deliberation, then set down her glass. She thrust her fingers through her hair, angered further by the spikiness of its appearance, and by the knowledge that she was looking far from her best. That anger fuelled the other. 'I'll tell you what's "with me" — whatever *that's* supposed to mean. I see no reason to be pleasant to the people who are out to destroy Oakham Manor and all that it means, and has meant.'

'We're not out to destroy the Manor.'

'That's not the way I see it!'

'You don't even know what we want it for.'

'So tell me!'

He hesitated, staring at her uncertainly, and then he shrugged, smiled slightly. 'It's no great secret; no reason why you shouldn't know. The meeting in Paris was big business; preliminary talks with some European firms.'

'What's that got to do with Oakham Manor?'

'*Patience*! I was telling you earlier, before we got side-tracked. The discussions in Paris were important, but I'm not centrally involved, really. Yesterday I came back to follow up some agency contracts. That's why I was in London, and happened to bump into you—'

'*Happened*?' The word was out, surprisingly, before she could stop it.

Neil Bradon hesitated, then grinned sheepishly. 'I . . . I was passing. I knew your case was on . . . Anyway, the point is when we come back to the Manor in a few days, to carry on the discussions Torrance is setting up, a decision will be made.'

'About Oakham?'

'That's right.'

'What kind of decision?'

Bradon hesitated once more. He eyed her carefully, as though weighing her in the balance, wondering whether he could trust her. Then he said, 'John Torrance is involved in negotiations with several firms in Europe. There are certain advantages . . . Have you ever heard of the gallium arsenide chip?'

'The *what*?'

Bradon smiled. 'In the world of information technology I guess you've heard of the silicon chip. It comes from sand.

It's available, and cheap to produce — and it's widely used. But the future for information technology lies with the gallium arsenide chip.'

'And where does that come from?'

'Gallium is extracted as a by-product of zinc and aluminium. Gallium arsenide is a compound of gallium and arsenic.'

'So?'

'Its great advantage over the silicon chip is its ability to transmit information exceedingly fast. The trouble is, if a company is to get into the market it will need to have access to certain industries, to make the new chip successfully and cheaply. Arsenic is produced as a by-product of copper, lead and other ores. It means that if a company such as CADS is to thrust strongly into this developing field it needs to get a toehold in zinc, aluminium, copper and lead industries.'

'And it can't do that?'

'Not in the States.'

'Why not?'

'Two reasons.' Neil Bradon scratched his cheek thoughtfully. 'First of all, since the signs are out, the companies CADS would wish to buy into have pushed their share prices through the ceiling; in other words, we're being frozen out. They stand to make more money if we have to buy at their prices. It's not the way John Torrance works.'

'And the second reason?'

'Anti-trust laws. Torrance could well fall foul of the US legislation against monopolies, or monopolistic operations. So even if he did get a stake in US companies he might still get clobbered.'

'So the answer is Europe?'

'That's right. We need to make a deal with certain companies in Europe. There's still room for swift and natural expansion in the field but we have to move fast. In the States our competitors maybe have the edge right now; but by coming into Europe the gloves are off. Torrance can build big with his own resources, once he pulls in these companies. But he can do even better if he can persuade the EEC to make an investment, through the European firms. If that happens, if he can bring them in on reasonable terms, and if he can get government and EEC support, he can turn the tables on US competition. He can freeze them out, and a major investment can be made, industrially, in Europe. CADS, with its allies, could become the biggest information technology operation in the Western hemisphere.'

'That sounds . . . big.'

'It is.'

'That leaves me somewhat puzzled.'

'How do you mean?'

'What's all this . . . big wheeling and dealing got to do with Oakham Manor?'

Neil Bradon looked vaguely uneasy, perhaps with the realization that he had talked too much of the affairs of CADS; perhaps for another reason. 'I . . . I suppose it's the result of my advice. You see, I'm aware, as an advertising man, of the importance of image-building. The Americans, they have their own image-building devices, but they don't apply to the same extent here in Europe. This is a long way from the States as far as attitudes are concerned; what goes big there doesn't necessarily happen here.'

'And what,' Tina asked coldly, 'does Madison Avenue wisdom suggest will *happen* here?'

'Europe is proud of its history and heritage — America is envious of that. You've earned it; we've yet to get it. So, Madison A venue *experience* — *though* you might sneer at it — suggests to me that what John Torrance needs as much as anything is the right image in Europe. If CADS picks up the other companies, there's got to be a base for the operation. All right, it could be a glass-walled skyscraper in Brussels or Berlin; it could be an architectural wonder in Luxembourg or Lausanne. I think that would be wrong.'

'A sense of history.'

'Right. The European venture will be big. People don't like . . . they even distrust . . . big companies. And glass walls, they make you think of people without faces, factory-like systems. It's not *European*, not in the sense it ought to be. I talked to Torrance, and we thought about chateaux on the Loire, but they're too fairy tale. We discussed castles on the Rhine, but there's something militaristic about them that could, again, produce the wrong image. And then we came across Oakham Manor, when we picked up a small firm that held the option.'

'You intend to use—'

'Torrance saw it straight away. It's reasonably accessible and yet has a touch of remoteness. It has a long history, it has an aged beauty, it has mists and meadows, romance, that curious kind of ethereal quality that few houses can ever possess. It has *roots*. And that's the kind of image that CADS in Europe needs to develop. An English country house image: solid, dependable, grand but not brash, fine but not thrusting. Oakham Manor has it, and I've persuaded John Torrance—'

'*You've* persuaded him!'

'He didn't need much persuasion. He's already—'

She rose to her feet and headed for the door.

It was still raining. As she hesitated in the doorway, Neil Bradon took her by the arm. 'What the hell's the matter with you? I just can't understand what you're so needled about! You know damn well Oakham Manor's out on its feet. Your father couldn't make it pay, couldn't maintain it. You've no private means—'

'You seem to know rather too much about my situation!' she flashed.

'Be reasonable . . . You'd be forced to sell off parts of the estate, as you've already done. Is that the way to save Oakham? If we took over, it *would* be saved—'

'For what? To become part of some ridiculous logo, some inane advertising campaign? Would you gut it to make office space? Would you "renovate" the terraces, make a new driveway, "improve" the view from the windows? Would you roll up in your ridiculously massive cars and wear tweeds and talk in your loud voices and forget all that the Manor has been, a home, a—'

Stiffly he interrupted her. 'There would have to be some changes, yes.'

'I *bet*!'

His fingers dug angrily into her arm. She made no attempt to pull away. She stared coldly at him; his brown eyes were hot with anger. 'It makes little difference anyway,' he said. 'You're stuck with some stupid, little girl dream that has no place in modern realities. Oakham Manor has been a great house, and Torrance will save at least some of that heritage.'

'*Image*, you said!'

'And for you, images aren't real! But what are your own views, and hopes, other than imaginings? Do you have any power to overturn the option we have on Oakham? Why do I even bother to talk to you—'

'Instead of Andrew McNeil Castle?' she interrupted fiercely. 'I'm sure you'd get a more receptive audience there. He's an American too, and has the same grubby attitudes about *reality* that you have.'

They stood glaring at each other, angry, hot, and in some incomprehensible way, excited. Slowly he released his grip. 'I don't think there's anything more to say,' he suggested quietly.

'You're damn right!' Tina said and ran out into the driving rain.

2

The Senior Planning Officer had not been pleased to have his holiday at Scarborough broken into by a recall to the colours for a planning inquiry in Morpeth. He had vented some of his spleen on Arnold, similarly recalled from his sojourn at Oakham Manor, to prepare the papers for the inquiry. Discussions with the Government Inspector beforehand had been difficult: his pin-striped punctiliousness had unsettled the Senior Planning Officer and had pushed Arnold into a mood of resigned despair. The outcome of the inquiry was in little doubt, but there were two weeks of exhausting summer days in a stifling committee room to be faced.

'I suppose *you'll* be going back to that place in Northumberland,' the Senior Planning Officer said bitterly. '*My* holiday plans are ruined, of course; it'll be impossible to get another booking now, and besides, there'll be no moving my wife. Her mother's due.'

His tone suggested he would prefer his mother-in-law was due for the drop rather than a visit but Arnold guessed it would in practice be the latter. He nodded. 'The task the Heritage Society gave me is all but finished now, as far as cataloguing is concerned. There are a couple of things I'd like to check further, but it should take me no more than five or six days . . . to the end of my holiday allowance, really.'

'Humph,' the Senior Planning Officer said.

'It's an interesting building in itself,' Arnold said, 'and I've found one or two things of importance. This, for instance — I've taken a copy of the original.'

'What is it?' the Senior Planning Officer asked reluctantly, peering at the document Arnold handed him.

'It's a builder's contract — for the construction of a tower at Oakham Manor,' Arnold replied, and then waited as the Senior Planning Officer laboriously read out its detail.

THE OAKHAM MANOR
BUILDING CONTRACT

This bille endentyd witnesseth that on the Tewesday next after the feste of Seynt Mathie Apostle the fourte yeere of Kyng Henry the Sexte A covenaunt was maked betwyn Thomas Wolfard on the one part ye and Richard Bangor and Adam Ambrynge masons on the other part ye, that is to sey that the fornsaid Richard and Adam shall make or do to make a towre joyned to the halle at Oakham fornsaid with foure botraies and one vice and tuelfe foote wide and sex foote thikke the walles, the wallyng tha tabellyng and the orbyng sewtly done after the towre of Deen well and trewely and competently a dore in the west also as good as the dore in the towre of Deen and a wyndowe of two dayes above the do re sewtly after the wyndowe of thre dayes of Helles. The fornsaid Richard and Adam shal werke or doo werke on the towre fornsaid two termes in the yeer saf the firste yeer, yeerly in the tyme of werking and settynge and leying that is to say bitwiyen the festes on the annuncyacion of our Lady and Seynt Michel Archangel but if it be other maner consentyd on both part ye. The fornsaid Richard and Adam shal take of the fornsaid Thomas Wolfard for the yarde werkynge XI scheelynges of lauful money of Inglond, and a Cade of full herrying eche ye er in tyme of werkynge and ech of hem a gowne of leuere ones in the tyme of werkynge so that they scholden be gode men and trewe to the werke fornsaid.

The Senior Planning Officer looked up at Arnold, in suspicion. 'They paid builders with *herring*?'

'Partly paid,' Arnold corrected.

'Probably more sensible than cash these days.' The Senior Planning Officer sniffed, more interested in the contract than he wished to appear. 'Well, I suppose it's something to have found an item of value for all the time you're spending up there. You'll be back in about a week, then?'

'Yes, sir.'

'Make sure. You know there's a lobby to deal with, up at Kielder again.'

Arnold gave him reiterated assurances.

* * *

The return to Northumberland sharpened Arnold's sense of appreciation of that area; the days he had spent at Oakham had been pleasant, and he knew he would again feel the anticipatory excitement he always experienced among the peles and castles of the northern coast. Additionally, there were other compensations. The small pub at which the Heritage Society had arranged accommodation for him appealed to Arnold. It was six miles distant from Oakham Manor, and reached by winding, twisty lanes, russet and green and flaring with occasional bouts of colour from splashes of hedgerow flowers. The pub itself had been by-passed twenty years earlier by a new road; now it lay on an island, huddling as though for protection behind a copse of trees and backed by farmland, while just two miles away the relentless motorway roared past, day and night. At the pub there was just a faint hum, an echo of the roar, and the rooms were high-ceilinged and spotless, there was a mockery of oak beams in the lounge bar which brought a smile to Arnold's face, and the locals had weather-beaten faces with manners to match:

tough, experienced, regular drinkers who had little to say and knew where they were. And while the landlord was big, pot-bellied and a trifle bellicose on occasions, his wife was largely friendly, apple-cheeked, and an excellent plain cook.

But when Arnold returned from his stint back in the Planning Department she had been apologetic.

'I'm awful sorry, Mr Landon, but you wasn't exactly clear about when you'd be coming back, was you? Thing is, we had a wedding party in from London last weekend, and then there was this other booking yesterday, we had to sort of turn things about, know what I mean? Anyway, fact is, we had to put a Mr Enright in the room you had — I know you liked it but we couldn't exactly ask Mr Enright to change, could we, specially when he was asking to book for a week or more? So I've put you in Number Eight. Will that be all right?'

It was all right. There was little to choose between the rooms in fact, apart from the view from the window. Arnold's new room looked out over the back, beyond the old stable block that now served as garages, and screened by the dark copse of trees, whereas from his previous room he had been able to gaze across open fields, past the motorway, to the distant, crumbling walls of Walbur Priory, behind which, in the hollow, Oakham Manor was situated.

But it was not important, and it would have been unreasonable to disturb Mr Enright, whoever he was, once he had settled in.

The drive into Northumberland had been tiring, and Arnold was rather late rising next morning. It was almost nine thirty when he came down to breakfast and there was only one other person in the dining room. He was a slim, pale man with fair hair and quick-moving eyes. He was dressed in a dark sweater and grey slacks and he was reading a tabloid newspaper; he flickered an uncertain glance in Arnold's direction and managed a small, tight-lipped smile when Arnold greeted him.

'May I join you?'

The slim man looked around hastily at the other tables; none was now laid for breakfast. 'Of course,' he said, a trifle uneasily.

'My name's Arnold Landon.'

'Keith Enright.'

'Ah.'

'Pardon?'

'You have the room I previously occupied,' Arnold said with a smile. 'I'm in Number Eight, now.'

'I hope it's all right.'

'Fine.'

Enright smiled hesitantly; he seemed to want to talk, but found light conversation difficult. He folded his newspaper, stirred his coffee as the landlady bustled in and took Arnold's order of orange juice, boiled egg and toast, and then said, 'I don't know this part of the world too well. Londoner, you see.'

'Northerner, myself,' Arnold admitted. 'But it's quite pleasant, open countryside around here.'

'Maybe that's the trouble. Don't sleep well. Country air.'

'You here on business?'

'More or less.' Enright sipped his coffee. 'I do a fair bit of travelling.' He thought for a moment, his glance slipping around the room as though seeking inspiration. 'It's mainly in the cities, though. Not country.'

'What line are you in?'

Once more the words seemed to come with difficulty, only after considerable thought. 'Electronics . . . sort of.'

Arnold finished his orange juice. 'That's a closed world to me, entirely.'

'So what sort of business are you in?'

'I'm a planning officer. I work In Newcastle.'

'You here on holiday, then?' Enright asked.

'Not exactly. I have a sort of . . . interest in ancient buildings, and materials. I've been asked to come and do a kind of investigation of documents, that sort of thing.'

'As part of the job?'

Arnold's egg arrived. He tapped the top of it with his spoon. 'No, I'm doing it in my own time. Busman's holiday, if you like. But I enjoy doing it, and it's very interesting. I had to break off for a week, though, to go back and see to some matters at the office.' He began to pull away the cracked eggshell; the egg itself quivered nauseatingly. Arnold liked his eggs hard-boiled.

'So where are you doing this research into these documents?'

Egg yolk spilled down the side of the eggcup. Arnold shuddered. 'Oakham Manor.' He applied himself to the toast, eyeing the egg balefully. He could force himself to eat some of the hardened albumen, so as not to offend the landlady, but he would find it completely impossible to attack the yolk. It was congealing now, in a little puddle on his plate and he took a frantic bite at the toast, averting his glance. He looked up.

Keith Enright was walking away from the table, newspaper folded under his arm. He had slipped sideways out of his chair, moved almost soundlessly away from the table, and was heading for the door without a backward glance or a taking of leave. Arnold stared at his back in surprise. He thought over their brief, ineffectual conversation. There had been nothing in his remarks to which Enright could have taken offence, surely? Or maybe he also disliked runny eggs.

An undercooked egg seemed a suitable scapegoat for a failure in establishing human relationships so Arnold accepted it. It also provided another reason for not eating the offending article. Arnold finished his toast, ignored the landlady's stiff back when she removed the uneaten egg, and enjoyed his coffee. At ten he was on his way back to Oakham Manor.

* * *

On this occasion he took the slight detour he had contemplated several times. The crossroads on the hedgerow-lined track that led to the Manor showed a decrepit signpost, one of whose arms pointed to WALBUR. Arnold turned right and followed the winding lane until he emerged in the small hamlet he could see from the first room he had had at the inn, and which Mr Enright now occupied. It was not very interesting in itself, this small scattering of cottages, but the ruined walls of the ancient priory, with two substantial wings still standing, drew his attention. The early construction would have been twelfth-century, of that he was certain; one winding stair could perhaps be dated back to the fourteenth but the rest of the two wings was of more recent origin. All in all an interesting hotchpotch, and one he might take time off to look into. The county archives would probably hold something of interest about the priory.

He climbed on the gate leading into the priory and looked down the hill towards Oakham Manor. It was surprisingly close. Walbur Priory stood on a hillock, commanding a view of the countryside, and a stream ran through the dip below Arnold, meandering on to Oakham land, drifting past the craggy rise in the ground that began the ascent to the copse to the right, with the manor house itself nestling in the folded ground to the left. He hadn't realized the buildings themselves were that close — some four hundred yards, little more, separated the two buildings. Arnold sat there for a little while, thinking. A fleeting thought crossed his mind, too winged to be grasped and analysed, and now it was gone it was too late to hold it. He looked again at the configuration of the ground, but the moment had passed. After a little while, he got down from the gate and made his way back to the car.

The fleeting moment returned to him several times during the next few days, perturbing him by its dancing elusiveness. He could not pin it down; he did not see Keith Enright again at breakfast; and when John Torrance came back to Oakham Manor with his cavalcade once more, Arnold worked on in the library, expecting the American businessman to call on him, but he did not.

But then, business *was* business.

* * *

'Business,' said Andrew McNeil Castle, 'is time.'

'And time is a scarce commodity,' Paul Dorset added. 'It's the reason why we need to get issues resolved as quickly as possible.'

Castle adjusted his portly bulk in his chair, sipped his coffee and glanced around with an air of appreciation at the panelled dining room. 'Well, I've never been averse to reaching swift decisions.'

'So if you *do* take over Oakham, we'll be able to agree terms?'

Castle smiled wetly. He caught the glance of the passive but watchful Barclay, with his accountant's mouth, predatory as a pike. 'I'm not too happy about a straight cash deal. I've no great cash-flow problem; Oakham is my heritage. It's a matter of balance. But I could be persuaded that the future is better than the past, so if I could pick up a parcel of shares in CADS, well, now that would be more acceptable . . .'

'You don't know yet whether you will own Oakham,' Barclay demurred.

'I'm confident,' Castle replied. 'When the time comes . . .'

'Ahh . . .' Andre Chevalier leaned forward and smiled. 'We Europeans have a different outlook on life; time seems to us not quite so important. But I will accept we have much to learn and *have* learned from you Americans. Our views have undergone some change.'

'But not a sea change,' Torrance said and rose. 'Shall we take some cognac in the other room?'

'But of course!'

Torrance led the way, with Chevalier, Castle, Dorset and Barclay following him. In the library he watched as Peter Barclay moved across with the glinting decanter to pour a cognac for the managing director of the Paris-based conglomerate in whose offices they had already held several long, detailed meetings. Apart from Andrew Castle, these men had already fenced at length both at Paris and here at Oakham; Castle had been invited for dinner this evening.

Now, as the evening drew on to darkness and the long dark tables gleamed in the shadowed light from the table lamps, they settled back into easy chairs among the serried ranks of books, the tall shelves, the dry, dusty odour . . . Neil Bradon was probably right when he spoke enthusiastically of Oakham Manor as possessing the right image for the European operation; the library was having an effect upon Chevalier in a way the Paris offices had had little effect upon the Americans. A matter of style; of heritage. Even Andrew Castle was somewhat subdued.

'What's happened to Neil this evening?' John Torrance asked as he accepted a brandy from Barclay.

'Gut ache,' Barclay replied unedifyingly. 'Seems he picked up some kind of bug, here or in Paris.'

'American boys ought to stick to good old American tack,' Castle said sententiously. 'My apologies, of course, M'sieur Chevalier.'

'Anyway, he's laid up in his room feeling sorry for himself,' Dorset said. 'Not that we need him. I think his advice on corporate image is peripheral to the more specific issues that we need to hammer out. Mr Castle won't want to be bored with such talk, but we have some new proposals which we could perhaps go over with you first thing in the morning . . .'

Don't push, Paul, John Torrance thought to himself. Don't try too hard, not with a wily old bird like Chevalier. From here, Torrance could sip his brandy, remain part of the scene and yet feel detached. He could observe the others: the pompous, portly, self-satisfied Andrew Castle, confident he would soon claim his 'inheritance' and prepared to bargain it away for a few shares in Torrance's company. There was Peter Barclay, trying to make it clear that the company future lay in his hands, with his mastery of figures and accounts. Paul Dorset put his faith in a legal mind, an overall view of the business. His confidence seemed untouched, his slow drawl unaffected by the wine, the gentleness of his dark eyes unmarked by the feelings that undoubtedly crawled behind them. Torrance watched the two men, the 'Apostles' as Bradon called them, as they continued their eternal, sterile jostling for position.

Perhaps in this room he obtained clearer insights into them as human beings. Dorset's slow drawl was deceptive: he was a man of perception with a keen mind and a track record that demonstrated his astuteness in business terms. A slow-moving intellectual: that was the surface picture. But wasn't there a story about his navy service, of a man badly injured, an incident hushed up . . . ? Perhaps a moralist without morals; a man of surprising contrasts.

On the other hand, Peter Barclay showed his emotions in his face, until the accountant took over and impassivity was the watchword. He ran an audit on every man and woman he met. He had a swift, agile, committed mind that throve on competition, yet lacked the imagination to range beyond the immediately practical. Ambitious, ruthless, with a heart as hard as his eyes. A company man.

But these two, the Apostles, they were dealing with Chevalier. The Frenchman was not for rushing; he had a style bred in his background. There was something in Chevalier's manner that reminded Torrance of the man who had been working in this room earlier today — Arnold Landon. A quiet commitment; a quiet, confident respect for life. Chevalier was harder than Landon, tougher, more materialistic, more dangerous. He was a businessman, not a dreamer, a man who would use his knowledge in a way Landon never would.

And yet they had something in common, Chevalier and the planning officer from Morpeth. John Torrance permitted a faint smile to touch his lips. He regretted he had not had time to seek out Landon since he had returned to Oakham Manor. He had meant to, but these few days had been hectic: there had been so much to think about. And he could hardly afford to be sidetracked by the absurd, schoolboy romanticism in which he and Landon had indulged, that afternoon in the kitchens . . .

* * *

Stresses and balances and weights.

Arnold Landon had explained it to him, the amateur historian speaking to the successful businessman. It was all about stresses and balances and weights and in a little while he had demonstrated and proved the very fact.

The pendants had been in the wrong place, but Torrance's suggestion that perhaps this had something to do with the puzzle of *latebras et diverticula* had proved to be the key. Suddenly they were like two schoolboys, panting and excited at what was happening in the thrill of discovery.

They had paced, and measured and calculated. The time had flown past while they discussed, talked and compared their measurements. And when the hollow ringing of the flagstones had changed, they had traced the path of the sound; they had reached the smooth pillar in the corner, protected in the angle of the kitchen walls by the massive buttresses, and they had probed with penknives, dug into the crumbling mortar until Arnold had laughed aloud.

'Stresses, balances, weights!'

Then it had been amazingly easy. Two separate, balanced points; the two men thrusting with their shoulders, and then all the workmanship of a mediaeval master mason was revealed as the stone groaned, moved, inched outwards under the pressure of their shoulders until the narrow blackness of the aperture stood revealed. Arnold Landon had slipped inside to stir the dust of centuries, and Torrance had hurried away to procure a torch from Peter Barclay.

Within half an hour he and Arnold Landon had been standing in a narrow, thick-aired corridor, with the dust of hundreds of years choking them, and the beam of the torch playing over the walls that had not been seen for generations.

'There's nothing about this in any of the library papers,' Arnold had whispered.

'But there is, as you told me. This is the explanation for your passage about *latebras et diverticula*.'

'But what was the purpose of this passage? How far does it go? The air's fusty; there's no fresh flow—'

'A dungeon, maybe?' Torrance had suggested, feeling the years fall away from him like flakes of dead skin.

'I don't think so . . . I don't think so . . .' Something had prickled at the back of John Torrance's neck at that moment, and perhaps the same kind of atavistic fear had touched Arnold Landon too, for both men had felt the necessity to leave the black passageway. They had stood in the kitchens, closed the stone of the pillar, and looked at each other breathlessly.

'We'll say nothing about this to the others,' Torrance had said. 'We'll investigate it further, together, when I return from Paris.'

'But anyone coming down here will soon find it — the way we've scuffed the dust, the broken cement—'

'Who comes down here, for God's sake?'

'Only me,' Arnold had replied, grinning. 'And now, you.'

The conspiratorial nature of their conversation had excited them both, two foolish, ageing men. And so it had seemed to John Torrance in Paris, immersed in the problems of the negotiations for the European enterprise. Yet now he was back at Oakham Manor, although those ancient stone walls had not enclosed him again, he dwelled on different perspectives from those which had engaged him in Paris. He watched the two thrustful young men pushing for the attainment of a conglomerate proposal that would extend CADS into Europe, but he was recalling the excitement of those foolish moments in the kitchens and the tunnel, and he was remembering what Arnold Landon had told him, and taught him and shown him . . .

* * *

'*Most cunning workmen* . . .' he said out loud, musing.

'What was that?' The other men were staring at him in surprise, as though they had forgotten he was there.

'Nothing,' John Torrance said after a moment. 'Just something I read, and haven't yet come to terms with.'

'Hmmm.' Castle humphed and set down his empty brandy glass. 'Well, I'd better be away. I thank you for your hospitality, and for the way you've kept Miss Vallance out of the way. It could have been embarrassing. As for the shares . . .'

'We can talk of that again,' John Torrance said coolly.

'I'll see you out,' Paul Dorset said, rising to his feet. After he and Castle had left, Barclay hesitated, caught Torrance's nod and then reluctantly made his own good-byes to Chevalier. He walked out, edgy as a cat, on the balls of his feet. In the silence that fell, Torrance was aware that Chevalier was watching him carefully.

Chevalier was a lean, elderly man with sharp eyes and an air of faded elegance that belied the keenness of his brain. He wore his nationality like a flower in his buttonhole and used it to effect, but he was as hard-headed as any tough American businessman, and as perceptive.

Torrance smiled. 'Are they pressing you hard, my friend?'

'Hard enough.' A glint of gold flashed in Chevalier's returning smile. 'They are persuasive young men who know their business.'

'They've learned in the hardest competitive schools.'

'But they have no experience of Europe.'

'Nor do I.'

Chevalier gave a Gallic shrug. 'That is so, but you have experience of the kind that comes only with age. Mr Barclay and Mr Dorset, they are *active*, they have dynamism, but there is something missing.'

'How do you mean?' Torrance asked quietly.

'I detect no *heartbeat* behind the proposals.'

Torrance considered the comment carefully. He was only half sure what the Frenchman meant and that meant he needed to move with circumspection. For his own mind was not yet entirely made up. 'Heartbeat . . . an unusual word to use in business negotiations.'

'But you know what I mean.'

Torrance shrugged. 'In the States we talk about gut feelings; the instinct that tells you a deal is right, that it opens up new possibilities, that it'll *work*.'

'It is near enough,' Chevalier said gravely. 'But not quite. I will tell you, Mr Torrance, your proposal attracts me. It has always impressed me with its possibilities. Now, I hear that the Japanese hope to have a mainframe computer running on gallium arsenide chips within twelve months and that Hewlett's have decided to speed up their research programmes. It underlines the need for decision, and speed.'

'I agree.'

'If you and I can reach agreement, the European nut is . . . how do you say . . . ? Ready for the cracking. My own French and Italian interests can come in; Anchédin in Switzerland will provide a Swiss-German conglomerate for the marketing side and have, additionally, access to copper and lead deposits and smelting facilities. I am already half . . . sold, is the word. But . . .'

'Yes?'

'But I had the feeling, in Paris, that you did not seem as committed as I had expected you to be.' Chevalier was watching Torrance carefully as he went on. 'Perhaps we French are different. Perhaps we are not so cool in the stage of negotiations. Anchédin is all but agreed; my fellow directors will follow my lead. Certainly, there are formalities, contracts, agencies, scientific research programmes, new company directorates, to be established and formalized, but these are but minor matters. But what is lacking is the heartbeat.'

'I'm still not clear.'

'Your aides have given me an excellent account of what developments in the gallium arsenide chip can mean for us all. But where is *your* commitment, Mr Torrance? CADS is John Torrance. And the proposals could be merely words.'

John Torrance suddenly felt naked. He sipped his brandy. He felt unable to respond immediately to Chevalier; the man was sharp, perceptive. His mind slipped away to

Arnold Landon, and to the book the man had shown him: *The History of Grisild the Second.*

The motives that may lie behind a man's decisions. He forced a smile on his thin lips. 'Heartbeats, gut feelings, they all become, in an old man's mind, merely the discomforts that occur after overindulgence in a good meal. I know the reply you wish me to make, my friend, but at this stage and at this hour I feel I cannot respond in the manner you think I should.'

He was aware of the veiled consternation in the Frenchman's eyes but he did not care. This was merely another of the charades he had played all his life and he was now beginning to see them as just that: charades. The odd thing was, as he looked into Chevalier's eyes, he saw shadows of understanding lurking deep in the man's glance.

'It's been a long day,' Torrance said apologetically.

Chevalier immediately rose to his feet. 'I quite understand, Mr Torrance.' He bowed, somewhat formally, and shook hands. 'I shall see you in the morning, before I leave.'

At the door he paused, and looked back, as though about to add something. Instead, impulsively, Torrance said, 'Do you believe in the lessons of history, M'sieur Chevalier?'

Chevalier quickly got over his surprise. He smiled. 'We are all merely extensions of our past. If we do *not* learn . . .'

After Chevalier had gone Peter Barclay returned attentively. 'Is there anything else, Mr Torrance?'

John Torrance shook his head. 'No. I shall read for a while. Then—' he glanced at his watch — 'then I've got some phoning to do.'

Barclay nodded, and withdrew quietly.

Torrance rose, walked across to the shelves and took down the book to which Arnold Landon had led him: *The History of Grisild the Second.* He read again the passage marked, then put the book back, turned down the lights as he left the room, and went to the drawing room. He lit a table lamp, selected a cigar. Soon, the aromatic smoke filled the room with its odour; he relaxed, sinking in his chair, thinking about the Apostles, Chevalier, Anchédin, Paris . . . and Arnold Landon.

He thought about them all for a long time, as the minutes ticked away and the phone sat mutely at his elbow. At last, he smiled. *'Most cunning workmen . . .'* he whispered to himself, and decided.

Slowly he picked up the phone.

* * *

The darkness was cold and oppressive. The air was thick and the atmosphere heavy with an ancient mistrust. The tiny red gleam of light, unwinking in the blackness of the passage, did little to illuminate but much to cheer: it gave a tiny island of colour and brightness, in a darkness that pressed down menacingly. The humming noise was almost indiscernible, yet his ears were attuned to it, waiting for the slightest change in tempo, the difference that could mean a decrease in quality.

It was a long time, a long wait, before the voice came out of the darkness. It fascinated him. Chilling, unearthly, it turned his skin cold with its quality, even though the words themselves meant nothing to him. They whispered down to him in the ancient darkness, sibilants from the tomb, he thought fancifully, and he marvelled at their sharpness, the distinct, albeit distorted nature of the sound itself, and he lit a cigarette to draw his mind away from the discomfort of the narrow place.

The intermittent glow showed him glimpses of pale stone, rough-hewn. He glanced at his watch and the luminous dial, against the cigarette glow, showed him his wait would not continue much longer.

The words slid on, pauses, silences, and at one point the almost shattering sound of a bell. He waited and the hour dragged past, and then there were other sounds, fading sounds, until the silence grew around him and he could stand no more and the red glow and the humming ended under his fingers, groping carefully for the switch.

'Hello, again.'

Arnold started and looked up in surprise.

Immersed as he had been in the building contracts which he was now busily cataloguing, he had not heard Tina Vallance enter. She was wearing a baggy sweater and jeans and her hair was tousled; she looked like a young, fresh-faced boy. He decided not to tell her so: in his experience women were unpredictable creatures, unable to take a compliment when one was meant and quick to seize upon insult when one was not intended.

'Good morning.'

'Working on a Sunday?'

Arnold shrugged. 'Another few days should see the end of the cataloguing; after that it'll be all downhill. There seemed little point in going back south for the weekend; they look after me very well at the inn, so I thought I'd put in some extra work here. You . . . you don't mind my working here at the weekend?'

She smiled. 'Don't look so anxious. Work when you like, I don't mind. After all, I maybe don't have the right anyway.'

'You've heard nothing yet from the court?'

'Judgment is likely to be delivered on Monday, I'm told. My solicitor is less than confident about the likely result.'

Arnold frowned. 'From what you've told me, it could all depend upon a certain nicety, in legal terms. The pity is, there was a falling off in standards, you know.'

'How do you mean?'

'Mediaeval manuscripts, documents, charters, even private papers, they all held a degree of precision that seemed to fade in later centuries. It may well have been due to the rise in literacy as time went on: originally, it was the clergy and the sort of official scribes who dealt with written matters. Later, as the number of people who could write grew, there was a deterioration. It means you can place absolute reliance upon twelfth-century written evidence; rather less upon fifteenth — and sixteenth-century materials. Politics crept into it too.'

'I don't think there was any question of politics involved in Oakham Manor matters.'

Arnold smiled. 'There's such a thing as *family* politics.'

'How could that affect documentary title?'

'Land has always been the most precious commodity of all in England. English Law has always recognized that land is the one immovable — the concept of real property concerns the right to hold the *res*, the thing itself. Building on that land strengthened title to it, in a sense, but ownership of the land remained, whatever happened to the building. And within families, it meant the land should not be split up into small parcels — so the eldest son inherited.'

'Except that in the case of the Wolfards, an accident of timing led to the younger son taking the land,' Tina said. 'Which effectively cuts me out.'

'So it would seem.'

'But you were saying about family politics . . .'

Arnold nodded. 'Yes. There are cases on record of . . . shall we say . . . a tampering with recorded fact. The primary historical source, for instance, apart from legal documents, is the parish register . . . births and deaths, that sort of thing. Take the position of the clergy in mediaeval times: the living might well be in the grant of the lord of the manor. The parish priest often did as he was told.'

'Falsifying a record?'

'It's happened — where pressure has been put on, for a particular family reason, such as concealment of birth. You know, paternity of a family's housekeeper's child, that sort of thing.'

'But how can that be proved?' Tina asked.

'Almost impossible — unless there's other evidence.'

'The Wolfards—'

Arnold held up a hand. 'I didn't say it might apply in your case. And you tell me there is a legal document.'

'A conveyance, yes. And a parish record of my ancestor's death.'

'That would sound solid,' Arnold said regretfully. 'As I told you earlier: at that time, documents were drawn up with much care.' Tina nodded disconsolately and moved away from the table, glancing along the bookshelves. He watched her for a few moments: he felt sorry for her, for she clearly loved Oakham Manor and it was the kind of love Arnold could understand and appreciate. She was probably wrong, thinking she would be able to continue to run the place without capital, but at least she would treat it with the respect its age and history entitled it to expect. The American company, that was a different matter. What would they do with it?

Almost as though she had divined his thoughts, Tina suddenly said, 'Torrance is advised that he could probably use the Manor as a form of headquarters, cum country club, cum business conference centre, cum image-builder, with the central emphasis upon the last. Do *you* think that would be bad for Oakham, Mr Landon?'

Arnold considered the question carefully. 'I'm not entirely certain. Old houses have been saved . . . although commercialization has destroyed the ambience of many. So, it depends, I suppose.'

'I distrust Americans instinctively,' she said.

'Mr Bradon seems pleasant enough.'

75

She flashed him a quick, hostile glance, startling in its severity, and he realized she thought there was some barb behind the innocent remark. 'Did you see me talking to him this morning?'

'No, I'm sorry . . .' Arnold was confused and showed his confusion. It touched her, and colour stained her cheeks. She half turned away, and in an offhand manner, she said, 'He . . . he's all right, I suppose, but a bit too brash and . . . and Madison Avenue for me. And he's wrong about Oakham; I think this company thing could damage it irretrievably. If *I* have any say in it . . .' She hesitated, shook her head, unwilling to get on that unhappy track again. 'He was telling me you discovered some sort of priest's hole at the Manor. You must show it to me some time; I know of nothing of the kind, certainly.'

'*Bradon told you what?*'

She stared at him, taken aback by his tone. 'You found a priest's hole, a hiding-place of some kind. Isn't it true?'

Arnold felt as though he had been kicked in the stomach. It was ludicrous that he should be affected in this way, foolish, immature and unnecessary. It was all so unimportant. And yet, when he had met John Torrance and they had made their discovery, they had both felt the same school-boyish excitement. Torrance had asked him to promise to tell no one, until they could both return and investigate further. The American had seemed to enjoy Arnold's company; to warm to him, as Arnold had to Torrance. They had had a *secret* — but even though Arnold had waited patiently, stayed away from the kitchens until Torrance could find time to join him and work with him, not only had Torrance not bothered to do so, but he had told one of his aides about the discovery. It was trivial to him, and it *was* trivial, unimportant.

But Arnold suddenly felt very lonely. 'Are you all right, Mr Landon?'

'Oh, quite well, thank you. I . . . well, I was surprised that Mr Bradon should know about it. I can't imagine . . . well, no matter.' He gathered his wits. 'It's not a priest's hole at all, not in the sense the term was used in the sixteenth century. I don't really know what it is, in fact. There was a hint, you see, in the early building documents that the mason was building in a peculiar way to accomplish certain designs which involved hiding-places and *diverticula*, but beyond that—'

'You mean it's a secret *passage*?' Tina said, her eyes shining. 'I never heard anything of that sort located in Oakham!'

'I tell you, Miss Vallance, I don't know what it was for — or even if it was a passage at all. I've only been there on the one occasion and—'

'Only the once? I thought you had a romantic streak, Mr Arnold Landon! Why haven't you been back there since?'

Why indeed, thought Arnold with a hint of sourness. He saw the excited enthusiasm in Tina Vallance's face and it warmed him. 'Have you got a torch?' he asked.

* * *

In the kitchens, she immediately asked him the obvious question — so obvious it had not occurred to him at all. Why on earth would there be a secret hiding-place in the kitchens — and how could it possibly remain secret? It took just a few seconds' thought for Arnold to come up with the answer, and once again it was provided by the building itself. He showed her the line of post holes in the stone floor. He explained that whatever the entry had been used for, its location in the kitchens would have meant that entry to it would have been easy and open. While on the other hand, the post holes demonstrated that some kind of screen had been erected there, behind which entry to the doorway would have been possible. It could have been an arras, but Arnold was inclined to believe that it would have been a wooden wall, serving as a screen, perhaps a false wall. Much depended upon the purpose for which the hiding-place — if that was what it was — had been used.

When he applied the pressure of his shoulder to the stone pillar and the stone moved, she caught her breath in excitement. There was a fetidity, a sweetness and sickliness about the air that gushed out; he did not recall it from the occasion of his first visit. Using the torch, he showed her the entry, then stepped inside with her following him closely.

They stood in the narrow, torchlit darkness of the chamber behind the pillar. When she expressed her excitement, her voice quavered.

Arnold could not feel excited. For her benefit, he flashed the torch around the narrow chamber, pointing to the far wall and what seemed to be a clumsy attempt at bricking up, with no attention paid to camouflage. It was clear that the chamber had extended into another passageway —perhaps the *diverticula* of the documentation — and that if that were taken down there would probably be some exit, either into a room of the Manor, or else out to the exterior walls, a method of secret egress from the house. But its purpose, he explained, could not be identified at this time.

'You're very grave and serious,' Tina complained mockingly. 'I think this is marvellous! So exciting! All these years, undetected, and now we're the first, perhaps for centuries . . .'

John Torrance had expressed the same kind of feelings, a barely repressed enthusiasm on his part. But it had passed, as it had passed for Arnold now, for in some curious way he felt betrayed by the American. And the chamber no longer held the same interest for him; perhaps he was being childish, but in some vague way he felt that it had been defiled.

Because someone else had been here, apart from Torrance, himself, and now, Tina Vallance. He *felt* it, almost physically; there was a taint in the air, something familiar and yet unrecognized, and in a flash of impatience he swept the torchlight around the narrow chamber. He caught the flash of silver and he stopped, bent down, picked it up.

'What's that?' Tina asked him.

Arnold shook his head, and put the small piece of tinfoil in his pocket. 'Nothing.'

She was standing beside him, caught up in the excitement of it all, but a little scared, too, by the close darkness and the age of it all. Her voice faded to a whisper. 'Do you hear something?' she asked.

He listened. He remembered the last time he had been here, waiting while John Torrance went for the torch. He had said nothing to Torrance on that occasion, but the hairs on the back of his neck prickled again now at the memory — or was it that he too could hear something now? Tina was touching his arm nervously. 'What is it?'

For a few moments he could still hear nothing, and then it came to him, a slight, sibilant scratching sound, faint and indistinct, unsteady, uneven; there was a rustling sound, and then it began again, the faint scratching, as though an animal was patiently scraping away for food, or to seek an escape from the confining darkness. Arnold swept the narrow chamber with the light.

The stone floor was dusty, though marked darkly in the corner; apart from that, there was no sign of anything untoward, and there was certainly nothing that sought to scurry away from the searching light. But the sound persisted and Tina nestled closer against him.

'*What* is *it?*'

Uneasily he answered, 'I don't know. I can't see anything but it sounds . . . well, as though there's mice, or a rat—'

'*Rats?*' She backed away from him, stumbling, and then reached for the doorway, scrambled through hastily. Arnold turned and followed her and when he came out into the kitchen he could see that she was trembling slightly. Shamefacedly, she said, 'I'm sorry. That was panic.'

'I quite understand.'

'*I* don't. Brought up at Oakham, I shouldn't be scared of the odd rat, but they're creatures I could never abide.'

'Nor I,' he confessed, to put her more at ease, and he applied his shoulder to the stone pillar, easing the slab back into place, closing the chamber once more. He was not afraid of rats at all, but there was something about the chamber that had made him uneasy the first time, and he had been glad to follow the girl out now.

He was getting old, and fanciful and foolish, and he was irritated by the ache in his chest, the residue of John Torrance's betrayal.

4

In the early morning, the cat came slinking out of the hedge-row, eyes gleaming with frustration at its unsuccessful hunt. It leapt lightly into the long grass, hesitated, its tail moving slowly from side to side as it raised its head, searching for the warning, and then, suddenly, it took flight, headlong into the roadway, regardless of safety. The bicyclist, a farm labourer late for work, caught the gleaming eyes in his bicycle lamp, and hastily applied his brakes: the road surface was damp from the light rain that had fallen before dawn and now his smooth tyres skidded and he fell, rolling into the long grass, bruising his shoulder, barking his knee, and he lay on his back there for a moment, cursing the grey sky and the star-tled cat. Then he struggled to his knees, pressed his knuckles into the damp grass to rise to his feet. He stopped, foolishly, kneeling there while the slow pace of his blood quickened with incredulity, which suddenly changed to panic. He rose, grabbed his machine, and in spite of the twisted handlebars, rode to the farm faster than he had ever done before.

* * *

It was almost midday before Detective Inspector Carter arrived at the scene of the cat's startled leap and the farm labourer's accident. The cause of their surprise still lay in the ditch, and the forensic lads were still at work there. Sourly, Carter noted that the local police had done little enough to prevent a certain amount of trampling around the scene of the incident, and he had no doubt that this would be another of the messy cases he had had to deal with of late.

He walked across to the police sergeant who had put the call through when the first report had come in from the farm and he took out a cigarette, lit it, and glanced, sourly at the sergeant. 'Woman?'

'No, sir. Male. Slim feller. About forty, I'd say; bit less, maybe.'

'Knife? Gunshot?'

'Not that I could see,' the sergeant replied. 'Head wound. Battered maybe.'

'Humph. Forensic will have to tell us, then. Don't like batterings; head wounds. Knives, guns, stand a better chance of laying hands on the villain, is my experience. You haven't kept the place very clean,' he added sourly.

'Couldn't, sir. The labourer was first; when he told his employer, *he* had to come take a look after he phoned us. Was here, with the labourer, when we arrived. Did their own bit of looking around for clues.'

'Bloody amateurs . . . What did they expect to find? Hell, if *coppers* don't know what to look for what the hell do these characters think they'll find? Killer's name and address?'

'Natural reaction, sir.' The sergeant caught the gleam in Carter's eye. 'Not that I condone it, of course. Already had a word with them. But Joe Stearns — that's the labourer chap — he did have something to say.'

'What?'

'The body in the ditch . . . Stearns thinks he's seen him, knows his face.'

'He *knows* him?' Carter said impatiently. 'Well, why the hell—'

'Not *knows* him, sir; seen him. Drinking at a local pub. The Red Lion.'

'He's sure of it?'

'Not sure. The man's not a local — Stearns reckons he fancies he's seen him at the Red Lion because he's staying there. Not from around these parts.'

More's the pity, Detective Inspector Carter thought sourly, and walked across to prise whatever information he could from the Home Office man in the ditch who, like all forensic scientists, would be full of *ifs*, *buts* and *maybes*.

And who would write a book when he retired about all the crimes he had solved.

CHAPTER THREE

1

The afternoon sun streamed in through the library window and Arnold took off his jacket to work in his shirtsleeves. It was not something the Senior Planning Officer would approve of, but Arnold was a long way from the office in Morpeth and a little licence would not go amiss. He could not settle today, for there had been much distressing activity at the inn. He had arisen early for breakfast and had been forced to endure the gossip of the landlady. She had been concerned, she averred, at the curious failure of Mr Enright to return to his room overnight; he had made no appearance at breakfast-time yesterday, and then there had been the visit of the local police early this morning, asking questions. Round-eyed, she had announced that they had discovered Mr Enright in a ditch a few miles away, and would be returning later to ask more questions, once the body had been transported to the nearest forensic laboratories for further investigation. There was no doubt they would wish to talk to Mr Landon. After all, he had had the room before Mr Enright, hadn't he?

Arnold saw no logic in the remark and the thought of interrogation by the police gave him twinges of dyspepsia; he had already gone through that particular mill before, in

Northumberland. It was not one of his more cherished memories. So he had fled, quickly, once breakfast was over, to the quiet of Oakham Manor, and had ensconced himself in the library where he was among old familiar friends.

Yet even they disturbed him. In particular the building contract for Oakham Manor. He had almost completed the work he had been asked to do for the Heritage Society, and was now largely pursuing interests of his own before he finally completed the task. But in pursuing those interests — the cleft oak beams he suspected had been used in the roof supports of the original building, the relationship of Oakham Manor to the structure at Walbur — he had been oddly bothered by the terminology of the building contract he had shown to the Senior Planning Officer that day in Morpeth. It might have been the disturbance occasioned by these investigations looming into Enright's death — and it must be apparent to everyone that Arnold Landon could offer no help in *that* direction — but Arnold simply could not concentrate on the materials spread out before him on the tables. Instead, his mind kept drifting back to the building contract, in a most irritating manner.

He spread it open in front of him and read it yet again.

This bille endentyd witnesseth that on the Tewesday next after the feste of Seynt Mathie Apostle the fourte yeere of Kyng Henry the Sexte . . . The fornsaid Richard and Adam shal werke or doo werke on the towre fornsaid two termes in the yeer saf the firste yeer . . .

That would make sense and was explicable; the two masons who had been building the tower would presumably be spending their time cutting the stone for the tower during the first two 'termes' or two quarters, six months in all. Yes, that made sense. So did the 'orbyng' which was to be 'sewtly done' and the 'settynge and leying' that was to be done between the feasts of the Annunciation of Our Lady and the Archangel Michael. The time span would be about right for mediaeval masons, and yet there was something about that timing which bothered him. Arnold was confused, unable to concentrate properly and it irritated him: could it be something to do with the original building of the house, and the deliberate construction of hiding-places and passages fit for the design? *What* design? Why had the passageway he and Torrance discovered been built at all? And had such *diverticula* caused problems in the building of the tower by Richard and Adam, timing problems that Arnold had not yet grasped?

It was all so irritating, and frustrating. He was hot and sweating and annoyed with himself for being unable to think clearly when the stocky man in the faded blue suit walked into the library, slamming the door behind him.

'Your name Landon?'

Arnold stared at the man: he had short, bristling hair, arrogant eyes and a badtempered mouth. And he slammed doors — in other people's houses. 'I'm Arnold Landon.'

'Carter. We need to have a talk.'

'Why?' It must have been the heat and the frustration; the man's eyebrows drew together at Arnold's directness.

'*Detective Inspector Carter.*'

That still gave him no right to slam doors and be so intrusive into people's privacy. Arnold remained quiet. The bad-tempered mouth twisted. 'I'm making inquiries into the death of Mr Keith Enright. I believe you might be able to help in those inquiries.'

'I can't imagine why.'

'You knew him.'

'No.'

'You'd *met* him.'

'Yes.'

They glared at each other antagonistically, Arnold hot and stubborn, Carter disliking instinctively any man who would work in a library on a hot summer afternoon. Carter extracted a small notebook on to the table in front of him and sat down. He scratched at his thatch of hair. 'You'd be well advised to cooperate.'

'Am I being uncooperative?' Arnold was alarmed at his own temerity; Carter was surprised at it.

'All right, let's start again. You knew Enright.'

'Met him,' Arnold corrected. 'And then only briefly.'

'In what circumstances?'

'I sat at his table for breakfast.'

'Because you wanted to meet him?' Carter asked swiftly.

'Because I wanted breakfast. It was the only table laid.'

Carter expressed disbelief by sniffing loudly. He made a note in his notebook, then glowered at Arnold. 'You talk to him?'

'Yes.'

'What about?'

'Very little. As I recall, we merely exchanged our names and—'

'Activities?'

Arnold hesitated. 'I think so. I told him I was doing some research. He told me he was an engineer.'

'Engineer?'

'Well, something like that. Ahh electronics, I seem to recall.'

'What happened then?' Carter asked truculently.

'Nothing.'

'What do you mean?'

'Well, my egg arrived.'

Carter was breathing heavily, waiting as though he expected some further explanation. Arnold did not feel he could give it; after all, his recollection of the situation was that Mr Enright had been upset by the sight of runny yolk. In the present circumstances it seemed hardly the sort of additional comment that would settle Detective Inspector Carter into a peaceful frame of mind.

'What,' Carter said after a long pause, 'happened after your . . . egg arrived?'

Arnold began to sweat even more; the room was becoming stifling with the presence of this objectionable police officer.

'Nothing. He . . . he left.'

'Without saying anything more to you?' Arnold wriggled under the lash of Carter's scorn. 'He said nothing more at all. The . . . the egg made me feel queasy. When I looked up, Mr Enright was walking out of the room. He didn't even say goodbye, or good morning or anything. He just went.'

There was a long silence. At last, Carter said, 'That seems very odd.'

Not if you'd seen that egg, Arnold thought.

* * *

Detective Inspector Carter did not regard himself as a man to be trifled with. Yet he had the feeling that this fellow Landon had trifled with him. He suspected that Landon was, essentially, a mild-mannered man, a bookworm, a person who would be more interested in the ancient past than the present, or even the future. Such men Detective Inspector Carter could eat for breakfast.

Normally.

Maybe it had been the library. He was not at his best in such academic surroundings. Life lay outside, in street brawls, seamy nightclubs, back rooms of pubs, and in this case a ditch — except that that wasn't life, but death. Even so, a library was not Carter's scene at all, and maybe that was why he had been less than effective with that chap Landon.

Even though he had known, intuitively, that Landon hadn't told everything he had known. True, what he had said so far was accurate and had been in line with what the landlady at the Red Lion had told Carter. She'd only seen Landon and Enright together once — at the breakfast table, and then for only a short while. They couldn't have said *much* together. Even so, a runny egg . . . ?

Carter shook his head as he walked down the broad stairs of Oakham Manor. That man Landon was one to be watched. He didn't want to talk to the police; he insisted he had no information to give; he claimed to be so immersed in his research as to be useless in any further inquiries. But even his research was something he had been reluctant to talk about: Carter possessed certain instincts after his years in the Force, and instinct told him Landon knew something but was holding it back.

It remained to be seen what the other denizens of Oakham Manor had to say.

He had already seen the girl, the young woman who owned the Manor — though she seemed somewhat evasive about that as well. She knew nothing of Enright; never met him or heard of him, had no idea why he should have been found in the ditch. Or why Carter should have come to Oakham Manor on his inquiries. She hadn't asked about that. Maybe she knew. Maybe she had something to hide too.

Suspicion. Occupational hazard.

The young man in the grey suit was waiting at the bottom of the stairs. 'Detective Inspector Carter?'

Carter admitted as much.

'I've conveyed your request to Mr Torrance. He's in conference in the drawing room but is prepared to see you immediately in view of the circumstances.'

Carter nodded and followed the slightly obsequious young man across the hallway and into the drawing room. There were three youngish men standing there; the fourth was seated, and older. He smiled faintly at Detective Inspector Carter. 'I'm John Torrance. This is Paul Dorset . . . Peter Barclay . . . Neil Bradon . . . How can we help you?'

Young, tough, American businessmen, bustling to get on, eager to please, but each with the hunger of a predator in his eyes. They would follow the lead of the man in the chair, they would obey the wishes of that man — but they would have secret thoughts churning inside their individual heads, ploys to be established, gains to be made, personal self-aggrandizement to be sought for. Detective Inspector Carter was pleased with himself at the thought. They were different animals from the usual run of petty criminals that he had to deal with. This whole affair could give adequate range to his not inconsiderable talents.

'Mr Torrance, I've come to ask a few questions.' John Torrance was raising an eyebrow: it was an affectation Carter disliked. 'It's about the death of a man called Keith Enright,' he blundered on.

'How can we help you?' Torrance asked again in vague surprise.

'Did he come to see you at all?'

'Mr . . . Enright?' Torrance shook his head slowly. 'I can't say that I've ever even heard of the name.'

'He was found dead in a ditch about four miles from here. Not far from the Red Lion, where he'd been staying for the last week or so, it seems.'

'Yes?' Torrance said politely.

'He'd been in the ditch for some hours. The back of his head had been subjected to a heavy blow . . . it killed him. Forensic are doing a job on him still, but we've got the general picture. We'll get more detail, of course . . .'

'Inspector—'

'He's not been here to see you?'

'Why should he?'

Carter wanted to say that he was here to ask questions not answer them, but there was something about John Torrance that quelled the words. He hesitated and turned to the dark-haired man called Barclay. 'Perhaps he came to see you at some time?'

The iron-hard mouth twitched in a vague amusement. Barclay shook his head. 'I can't imagine why. No, I've never met this guy.'

'And you, sir?'

Paul Dorset's eyes had a gentleness that did not fool Detective Inspector Carter: he'd once put away a wife-beater who had eyes and hands like this man. And the slow drawl sharpened Carter's nerves, when he replied, 'I know no one called Enright, and I can't guess why you think I should have known him. Just what—'

'Mr Bradon?'

This was a smooth one: good looking, well dressed, smart as hell and with honest eyes, the kind behind which you could think evil thoughts and set up bank robberies. The lifers in the jails always had honest eyes: funny thing, that.

'Can't help you, I'm afraid, Inspector.'

Torrance rose to his feet, walked across to the fireplace and locked his hands behind his back. He looked carefully at Carter, sharp old eyes weighing him up in a manner that made Carter uncomfortable. 'Just why do you think one of us might have met this man Enright, or even known him?'

'He was a Londoner, sir. But staying at the Red Lion.'

'A holiday?'

'Don't think so. But his stay here in the area has roughly coincided with yours.'

'How *roughly*?'

'I understand you've spent a period here, then went off to Paris, and now you've come back . . . Enright booked in just a day before your return, and said he'd be leaving in about a week's time. When I understand you'd be about to leave.'

The man called Bradon snickered. 'That's pretty rough.'

Torrance smiled gently, like a friendly tiger. 'I don't see how there's a connection in that, Inspector. There must be a number of holiday-makers in the area with a similar kind of schedule.'

'But they're not dead, sir.'

Torrance's glance hardened. 'I give you the point, Inspector, but—'

'There's a poacher up at Walbur called Riley, Mr Torrance. He's been in to see us.'

'Very public-spirited,' Paul Dorset murmured.

Recklessly Carter plunged on. 'He works in the woods at night, doing a bit of pheasant shooting. Small beer; not my interest, certainly. It's why he felt able to come forward. Because he'd seen this car, you understand.'

'What car?'

'Blue Ford.'

'Yes,' Torrance said testily, 'but I mean—'

'We found it about a half mile from where we discovered the body,' Carter interrupted. 'Its nose was stuck in the river. Can't say who drove it there, but it wasn't Enright.'

'How do you know that?'

'With a bashed-in head? No, he was killed and the car driven away and dumped. Just to delay matters, earn time.'

Torrance sighed and shook his head. 'I still don't understand.'

With a flourish, Carter drew his notebook from his pocket and consulted it gravely. 'These dates mean anything to you gentlemen?' He read them out and looked up; all four men were now giving him their full attention. 'They're dates when you were in . . . residence at Oakham Manor?'

Torrance nodded. 'Yes.'

'Anyone else here on those dates?'

There was a short silence; it held an edge of tension. Carter had the feeling no one wanted to speak and he felt the slow movement of an exultant excitement in his veins. Now it was their turn to feel uncomfortable. 'Anyone else?' he pressed.

John Torrance bared his teeth in an unwilling grimace. 'On two of those dates, certainly, we had a . . . guest, here at the Manor.'

'His name?' Carter rapped out.

'Chevalier.'

'Address?'

Paul Dorset moved forward protectively. In his slow drawl, he said, 'I don't see why you need it, but his office address is on this card, his personal address in longhand on the reverse.'

Carter took the card, slipped it inside the notebook. He looked around at the small, tense group. 'His business with you here at the Manor?'

'That's just it,' Peter Barclay said quickly. 'Business, that's all.'

'I don't think the detail need concern you,' Torrance agreed, setting the line they would all now follow. 'You still haven't explained about this poacher and finding the car—'

'Oh, *he* didn't find the car in the river. We did. But after we found it, he came forward. He'd seen it before, that's the point.'

The room was silent. They all wanted to ask the question, but three of them waited for John Torrance's lead. Carter looked at each of them in the lengthening silence: Bradon, Dorset, Barclay, and used all his knowledge of criminal natures to read what he saw in those faces. He prided himself on his knowledge of criminal faces, and businessmen, he knew, were among the biggest crooks of all.

'Your silence,' Torrance remarked in a tight voice that accorded with his whipcord frame, 'suggests to me you wish to make a big deal out of your next remark, Inspector.'

Niggled, Carter said, 'What remark would that be?'

Torrance sighed, but Carter wasn't fooled for he detected the tension in the man's hands. 'All right, Inspector, I'll ask the question. Where did this . . . poacher see the blue Ford car before?'

With great deliberation, Carter inspected his notebook again, then looked up. He had four faces to scrutinize, but only one pair of eyes. He concentrated. 'Well, on the nights in question, the nights I've just given you the dates of . . .' He glanced at each of them in turn. 'On those nights, the blue Ford car was parked just beyond the bridge.'

He looked at Neil Bradon. 'On Oakham land.'

He shifted the glance to Dorset, then Barclay. 'Within walking distance of the manor house.'

When Torrance shifted slightly, Carter allowed his gaze to rest penetratingly on the old man. 'And now Enright's dead, and the car was in the river. Are you sure, Mr Torrance, that you don't know anything about this feller Enright?'

* * *

It had been, he considered, a masterly piece of timing on his part. First, you allow your natural belligerence and lack of charm to unsettle the opposition: you got to know your own

93

faults when you started to probe the weaknesses of others. So, know your own faults, and use them. Right, when they're unsettled, you tease 'em a bit. Let their own imaginations run riot a bit, let 'em get a bit heated, scared, nervous . . . even if they're innocent as woolly lambs. Then, when the temperature is right, you shove it to 'em. Even if you've got very little to shove.

For what was there? A stranger to the district; he parks his car on certain nights on the property of local landowners where there's another party of strangers. Could be he was a night birdwatcher; could be it was all straight business at the manor house. But Enright gets himself killed.

Somewhere.

And the car is dumped.

And everyone in that drawing room in Oakham Manor is nervous as hell. They are not saying anything, but there was more than a bit of mental sweat in there.

Different from that character Landon.

Different. He just wasn't saying everything he knew, but what he had to say was probably unimportant anyway — it'd be tied up with that bloody library and would only confuse matters, no doubt. But those four in the drawing room . . . maybe it was just because they were Americans . . . different culture and all that, perhaps expecting bludgeons and third-degree or something . . . or maybe it was because they were businessmen, with all the secrets that businessmen always have to hide.

But that was the word. Secrets. All four of them were nervous as hell but there was more to it than that. There was something else in all that build-up of tension in that room. A secret. Secrets.

And by Detective Inspector Carter's count, at least two men in that room were not just worried. They were scared.

2

Upon reflection, Arnold considered he had behaved rather badly. It was true that he could find an excuse for his behaviour: he had been adversely affected by the boorishness of Detective Inspector Carter's manner. The man was an egocentric, arrogant, rude, self-opinionated bully, and any success he might have achieved as a detective was, Arnold was sure, purely accidental.

Nevertheless, Carter represented the law, and it had been wrong of Arnold to refuse, in effect, to be helpful. For now that he thought back to the occasion of his brief conversation with the demised Enright, Arnold considered that there might have been another reason for Enright's rapid departure. That reason could have been connected with the fact that Arnold was working at Oakham Manor, for immediately after Arnold had admitted the fact, Enright had risen, making no excuses, and left. Defensively, Arnold had blamed the egg; now, he was not so sure. And he should have told the detective about it. Arnold could not guess *why* Enright should have been disturbed to learn that Arnold was working at the Manor, but he had certainly left as soon as he discovered it.

And then there was the matter of the discovery Arnold had made in the kitchens. It could have no bearing on the case, but Carter *was* making inquiries at Oakham Manor, and Arnold had already been told, in Northumberland, that it was for the *police* to decide what was important, not the informant. Still, it seemed that Carter had also interviewed John Torrance so it was likely he had got the information from him. After all, Torrance had seen fit to tell others about the discovery he had made with Arnold, so there was no reason why he should not mention it to Carter. John Torrance . . . Arnold thrust the name to the back of his mind, dismissively. The thought of the betrayal still rankled . . .

He was waiting patiently at his allotted seat at the table in the County Record Office. He had inspected the file of holdings and made his selection; the officer in charge had not been pleased because, it seemed, the papers he had requested had not been the subject of search for many years and had been deposited in the building extension next door, which meant she had to leave her cooling coffee to get them. Arnold wouldn't have minded her finishing her coffee, but there was a balefuleyed supervisor in the next room and the assistant had marched stiff-backed to get the papers.

When she brought the papers to Arnold they were tied up with blue string in waxed paper. It was a curious way to keep old documents and hardly a safe method, but he shrugged mentally, having come across such aberrations before, and began to work through the papers. They consisted of deeds, land grants, conveyances, correspondence regarding tithes and then, as he worked back, longer, older, thicker documents full of convoluted legal phrases, dog Latin, Norman French and words beyond his comprehension.

But then he got his surprise. Walbur Priory had closed down some two hundred years ago, but its earliest recorded history was a document of 1549.

Before that, it had been in use as a nunnery. Arnold sat back, surprised. The conversion was unusual, but not unique. Nevertheless, for Walbur Priory to have been changed from a nunnery into a monastery, when only a short distance away a building erected as a monastery was converted into a manor house, was a situation that was clearly not of regular occurrence. He read on for a little while, but other thoughts drifted into his mind, the dancing, elusive memory that had teased him for some time and then, distracted by the hovering assistant who intimated it was near closing time, he placed the papers tidily inside their waxed package, gave the assistant some advice on the retention of valuable documents, and then made his way out to the car park and drove back to Walbur.

He had the beginnings of a theory.

* * *

He sat again on the crest of the hill above Walbur Priory, and the evening gathered about him, the shadows lengthening along the ground, creeping towards the copse and the slope and the bordering land of Oakham Manor. The lie of the land was now familiar to his eye and he was able to people it with its past activity — the meadows would have been down there near the winding stream, and the terraced hillside still showed patterns of the agricultural activity that had gone on there: even two hundred years would not destroy such patterns under a dying sun.

The theory could hold, fanciful though it might be, somewhat scurrilous though it certainly was. The configuration possibly supported it, but much would depend upon whether the lines of the hill among the trees were completely natural; and even more would depend upon what he found in the passageway at Oakham Manor.

If he even looked for anything.

A light breeze sprang up and his back was suddenly cold. There had been a few hours in the Manor when he thought he had found a friend — he had to admit that to himself now. More than a friend: a person whom he could admire for his own achievements, but who was able to learn still, listen to another's enthusiasms, bring to them a perception that the enthusiast might lack within his own excitement, and then share the breathtaking feeling of discovery. It had been there, he had felt it, and he was a man without friends, an essentially lonely man to whom a brief friendship could come as an unnerving experience. He had waited for Torrance to come back, to share the experience. He had not come — and he had talked about the passageway.

Their passageway.

Arnold smiled to himself. Childish. A step towards senility. All so unimportant. No matter; Torrance had had no real interest in the discovery after that first thrill, but that was no reason for Arnold to turn his back on it. Use the word disappointment, rather than betrayal. That would bring an element of balance into his feelings.

Even so, he felt twinges of regret. If his theory did hold water, facts would prove it; but he would have liked to have talked it over with John Torrance. He had *liked* the businessman. Still, Tina Vallance had been excited by the passageway and the chamber: perhaps he could test out his theory on her.

He made his way back to his car, and returned to the Red Lion and the chatter of the public bar. It was mostly about the murder of Keith Enright, so Arnold went early to bed.

* * *

It was mid-morning before Arnold left the library and looked for Tina Vallance. He tapped at the door of her apartments but there was no reply; he considered walking downstairs but became edgy at the thought of meeting John Torrance so he went back to the library. Standing disconsolately there he looked out of the window, and caught a glimpse of Tina in the gardens above the meadow. She was alone, standing with her hands clasped behind her back, looking out across the fields. She seemed, at this distance, very small and very vulnerable.

Arnold hurried down the stairs and made his way through the back entrance into the gardens. Box hedges screened his view but he made his guess and followed the long hedge which finally ended down near the stream that meandered towards the meadow. Tina was standing some thirty yards across to his left. She did not hear his approach.

'Good morning, Miss Vallance.'

She started, turned her head quickly to look at him. There was something odd about her eyes, a redness, an unnatural puffiness about her eyelids. 'Oh . . . Mr Landon.'

'I hope I didn't disturb you.'

'It's all right.'

'I saw you in the garden, alone, and thought ah . . . thought I'd come and have a . . . er . . . chat with you.'

She had turned her head away; she hardly seemed to hear him. 'It's peaceful down here,' she said.

'Yes.' Arnold hesitated, not certain whether she wanted to be alone, to enjoy that peace. 'Was it about anything important, Mr Landon?'

Arnold shuffled, aware of the sadness in the young woman's voice. 'Well, not really important. Just . . . I thought you'd maybe like to hear about my . . . theory.'

'With regard to?'

'The passageway.'

'Oh?' She turned her head to look at him, a hint of interest straining her tone, but overlaid with a general lassitude. 'You mean you've worked out what it's there for?'

'I can make a guess,' Arnold corrected her. 'But that's all it is, a guess. I'd need to do a bit more poking about down there, do some checking. It all has to do with the early history of the place, and its relationship with the priory at Walbur.'

'I don't understand.'

'At about the time the monks moved out of Oakham, the nunnery closed down at Walbur. The monks moved there.'

'So.'

'It was a reflection of the close contacts that had always been maintained between the two orders.'

She stared at him. 'I still don't understand.'

Arnold took a deep breath. 'Well, I think you have to remember that ideas of . . . well, vows in the church and so on, they were regarded a bit differently in mediaeval times. There was a tendency towards . . . transgression.'

'Surely not.' She raised her eyebrows. 'I understood they took religion very seriously. Excommunication, and all that.'

'Maybe so,' Arnold persisted, 'but at the same time there was a great deal of gossip about the lives of the celibate . . . or supposed celibate. Of course, much of the gossip would have been political — the need to root out rival religious sects, or discredit the Church of Rome — but there must have been some fire behind the smoke. Indeed, recent research among the French mountain villages discloses that women actually offered themselves to the local priests, and the husbands were quite complaisant about it.'

'Just what are you suggesting, Mr Landon?'

Arnold turned pink. 'Well, it goes back to the building of the abbey and its extensions, here at Oakham. I've told you I came across the instructions given to the monk Waiter, who was the mason responsible. He was to build *latebras et diverticula*, and we've found the passageway. But what was its purpose? I think I can now make a guess. The papers in the Record Office, and my own observations from Walbur . . .'

'What observations?'

'If you sit up there on the hillside, and look down to Oakham, you'll see there's a natural fold in the hill which is covered by clumps of trees. There's a line of sight, a regularity of line that suggests to me some kind of link between Walbur and Oakham — but I think it was more than just land con-figuration. I think when the extensions were constructed they were deliberately placed to take advantage of the porous rock foundations of that hillside.'

'A tunnel?'

'A tunnel; a method of egress. And my bet is the cham-ber and passageway under the kitchens is the entrance to the tunnel which, at some time in later centuries, was bricked up.'

'And its purpose?'

Arnold scratched his cheek, slightly uncomfortably. 'I think . . . if mediaeval gossip is to be believed . . . monks often forsook their vows of chastity and consorted with local ladies who had taken the veil.'

'You're not serious!'

'It's only a theory,' Arnold suggested lamely.

Tina Vallance smiled. 'How *scurrilous!*'

'Well, yes, it is a bit, but I think it's feasible. Men, and women, can be weak, and in those far-off days, well, there were often rumours of bastards born within nunnery walls, you know. It needn't always have been the gardeners who were to blame. Anyway, I thought you might be interested, and I . . . I'd like your permission to test the thing out.'

'In what way?'

'I could remove some of that brickwork, check where the tunnel actually goes to, how far it runs, where it might have emerged. Who knows? An exit might still be there, half buried under undergrowth.'

'I hardly think your theory—'

'It is quite serious, Miss Vallance, I assure you, and there's plenty of historical precedent. Gibbon, writing of Pope John XXIII, made my mind boggle many years ago when he wrote: *The most scandalous charges were suppressed: the vicar of Christ was only accused of piracy, murder, rape, sodomy, and incest*—'

'*Only!*' Tina said, half smiling.

'And then, in the nineteenth century there was the scandalous tale of the nunnery at Scorton, only one of a whole series of scurrilous stories about the Church—'

'Please, Mr Landon.' Tina Vallance shook her head, her features tinged with sadness. 'It's not that I lack interest in what you're saying; a little while ago I would have been excited at the possibilities behind what you're telling me, but now . . . Well, you can have my permission, of course, to work in the passageway but you'd better get your skates on to do the work you think is necessary. Because in a short while my permission will be more or less worthless.'

'What do you mean?'

She turned and began to walk back towards the manor house. Arnold walked beside her silently. He could guess what was coming, but he was reluctant either to leave her to walk back alone, or to question her further. In the event, the decision on how he should behave was taken from him. As they neared the edge of the box hedges a man stepped into view, barring their path. It was Neil Bradon.

He was staring directly at Tina Vallance.

He looked uncomfortable, and vaguely unhappy, but also rather annoyed as though he was struggling with emotions he did not wish to reveal. Tina stopped, stared at him, and then made to step past him. He put out a hand, touched her lightly on the arm.

'Yes?' she asked, coldly.

He hesitated. 'I . . . I . . . just wanted to say I'm sorry. I've just heard.'

'News travels fast,' she replied in a cool tone. 'You businessmen seem to have inside tracks . . . is that how you describe it?'

'I merely wanted to say—'

'Crocodile tears, Mr Bradon, become you no more than they do any other insincere predator. It makes not a damn bit of difference in the long run: the fate of Oakham Manor is sealed either way, isn't it? It doesn't really matter who owns it.'

'Even so, there's nothing insincere about my—'

'Spare me, please,' she said coldly, and brushed past his restraining hand to continue walking alone towards the house. Uneasily, Arnold remained with Bradon; the two men watched her silently as she made her way up the steps to the courtyard. As she disappeared, Bradon grunted softly; Arnold could not be certain whether it was occasioned by exasperation or relief.

'Well, that's that, I suppose,' Bradon said, almost to himself.

'I gather that the outcome of the suit in Chancery was not in her favour,' Arnold guessed.

Bradon glanced at him; honest, troubled eyes, they yet held secret depths that Arnold would never fathom. 'The judgment was handed down yesterday,' Bradon said. 'Her solicitor rang through this morning.'

'How did you come to know about it?'

Bradon hesitated. 'Simple enough — and not sinister. She will have no rights in the estate now; the solicitor for Andrew Castle was quick to get on the phone to tell us that future dealings over Oakham could now quite firmly be undertaken with him, on behalf of Castle.'

'Pity.'

'I guess so. I feel . . . sorry for her. But in a way, the die was already cast anyway, and as far as CADS are concerned, I suppose it makes things a bit easier. She'd have fought us, and that could have been costly, in time as well as money. And largely useless.'

'That's one way of looking at things,' Arnold murmured noncommittally. He began to move away; he had no great desire to spend time with any of these American intruders, in view of his experiences to date with them.

But it seemed he was unable to avoid them on this occasion. Bradon was trailing behind as he walked up towards the steps, but as Arnold reached the steps a man walked out of the courtyard and stood there, staring at him. It was John Torrance.

The lean, whipcord figure was tense. Arnold had seen soft amusement, and excitement in the man's mouth but now it was set like bent iron, grim and angry. The lines on Torrance's face were deep, harshly etched as he glared in Arnold's direction, hardly seeing or recognizing him. His eyes were narrowed, and dangerous. Arnold hesitated, opened his mouth to speak, but then the cold glance slipped past him, ignoring him, denying him status and interest.

'*Bradon!*'

The voice was low, and yet it cracked like a whip in the silence. Behind them in the trees a flurry of birds soared skywards as though disturbed by the harshness of John

103

Torrance's tone; Bradon's steps became more hurried as he hastened up the steps.

'Sir?'

'The others. Dorset; Barclay. Find them. I want the three of you. I want you now! Move it!'

He turned, walked away on stiff, angry legs. Arnold stared at Neil Bradon. The young man's face was pale, and his eyes were disturbed. But he was not surprised. For a moment, Arnold had the odd feeling that this was something Neil Bradon had been expecting, even counting on.

Then the young man had brushed past him, hurrying into the courtyard, and Arnold Landon was glad that he personally was far divorced from the pressures and tensions of the world of big business.

He would settle for history.

3

In the history of any corporate body, John Torrance thought bleakly, there comes a point when its head, its driving force, finally understands that his position has changed, perhaps irrevocably, and it is time to move out, relinquish the power he holds and make way for younger, more thrusting executives. The law of business was like the law of the jungle in that respect: he had always known it, and of recent years had become ever more conscious of it. And yet, like most men, he never believed it would ever happen to him. The reins would still be held tightly even when his hands were old, gnarled and weak. Until *he* decided to give them up, hand them over.

That presupposed he was prepared to fight; teeth and claws still ruled in the business jungle, and he was sure that his strike power was still more than enough to throw back any of these Young Turks, bleeding and defeated. But all that was beside the point, in a sense. There were rules, even while you went out to establish the best power base possible; rules to be followed, patterns to be obeyed in developing your strategy, and one of the basic patterns was the good of the company and the shareholders.

Deliberately, he let the silence grow around him. He took out a cigar, clipped its end, lit it, tasted the strong tobacco on his tongue and in his throat. The aroma reached his nostrils, soothed him, gentled his anger, but only to the point where it became controllable, usable and the more deadly for that as far as these three young men facing him in the room were concerned. They were now seated; he stood in front of them, legs braced, glaring at them as he slowly took the cigar from his mouth.

'Gentlemen, I've had disturbing news — and I want to know who's responsible for it.'

The three men were silent and tense. Paul Dorset's eyes were heavy-lidded, contemplative, but Peter Barclay's glance was nervous and quick as though he were seeking some means of escape from the room when the going got tough. Neil Bradon sat rigidly, stiff-backed, waiting. His hands were still; Torrance recognized the signs of control in the man.

'All right, fine, you don't know what I'm talking about,' Torrance said smoothly. 'So I'll put you in the picture, like you were all tyros and didn't know what the hell this business is all about. Because I sure as hell guess I'll get nothing out of any of you until I spin you a few facts. First, the obvious one: the whole basis of our venture into Europe is to continue CADS's growth through the European deals. Right?'

Paul Dorset nodded, almost sleepily. 'That's the company strategy.'

'Tied in with the whole thing, though, is the need for two things to happen. First, we have to keep a low profile on *what* discussions we're having, and with whom. If it's too obvious that we're dealing with certain people, like Chevalier and Anchédin, it can cause market flurries that could lead to a million dollar rise in share costs. We must buy into the European conglomerates as cheaply as we can: our own profitability depends upon it. And the second thing is, we've got to do our politicking gently, and easily, if we're to get EEC support for our venture.'

Peter Barclay nodded in agreement: Torrance could see he could guess what was coming.

'The main thing the European politicians are concerned about is that it must be seen that CADS isn't coming into Europe to make an American killing. We have to show good faith in our entry; we've got to show Europe that they stand to make as much out of it as we do. The gallium arsenide chip production by 1990 will be . . . what . . . ?'

'It'll be hitting two billion dollars,' Barclay supplied.

'It'll overtake silicon and will be established as the best, very large-scale material for fast information and communication technology by the end of the decade. And it's *governments* that will make the most use of the gallium arsenide chip.'

Torrance glared about him in the tense silence, and stabbed at the air with his cigar.

'European governments will need the chip for military requirements. They'll need it for the storing of information. But *we* know that business and consumer use for the chip has equally enormous potential. The marriage of government and consumer use will be irresistible to European business interests but we've got to come in clean!'

'Mr Torrance—'

'Wait!' Torrance's voice cracked like a whip. 'We can't slide in on a blood bath, a cutthroat, competitive situation which will simply end up with every European firm the poorer and CADS the kingpin with all the cash, the investment potential, the ability to survive and grow.'

'We've always seen ourselves as the *leaders*, sir,' Barclay demurred tightly.

'But not where the leaders go right through the battle unscathed and the rest of them get bloodied,' Torrance said grimly. 'It's one of the things you have been trying to persuade Chevalier about, in Paris and here at Oakham. Persuade him of our good faith. So, what I want to know right now is . . . who's playing the field, behind the smokescreen?'

The silence grew around them as Torrance stood glaring at them. Paul Dorset shifted heavily and uneasily. He glanced at Barclay, then towards Bradon. He shrugged. 'I'm not sure what you're driving at, sir. We thought we had convinced Chevalier that even if we were the leaders in the deals, he and the others would come out well. I don't understand what . . . what's led to this situation. What's going on, exactly?'

John Torrance drew on his cigar, and watched the three men who were closest to him in his organization. One of them had to be involved in this betrayal. He wouldn't have cared too much, except it *was* a betrayal. The words Arnold Landon had shown him flashed across his mind: *most cunning workmen*. He turned away angrily for a moment, flicking the ash from his Havana in a short-tempered gesture.

'What's going on, you ask,' he said, half snarling the words. '*Exactly*, I don't know. But in general . . . I have too many unanswered questions.'

Neil Bradon cleared his throat. 'You spoke of good faith, sir.'

'A precious commodity. And something we must demonstrate if we are to succeed in this European venture.' John Torrance paused, his eyes hooded. 'I've had a call in the early hours of this morning that makes me believe we're going to have trouble convincing our European friends, like Chevalier, that we can demonstrate good faith. The signs are that we — I should say *someone* — is out to make a killing.'

Paul Dorset frowned, and glanced at Peter Barclay. 'You mean . . . share-dealings?'

'Precisely.' Torrance let the word hang crisply in the air for a few seconds while he scrutinized the features of the three men he had trusted. 'Share-dealings. Not large, not extensive, but . . . important.'

'Chevalier knows about it?' Peter Barclay asked.

'*That* we'll be finding out tomorrow, I guess; and when we meet later in the week the questions will get asked. So, I ask the basic questions right now. *Who*?'

There was a short silence. Then Neil Bradon asked quietly, 'Isn't it equally important to ask why?'

John Torrance grimaced. 'I can make an educated guess straight away. Greed. The right purchases now, a flurry in

institutional buying when the news really breaks of the pro-
posed mergers, a rise in share prices, and our purchaser is
sitting pretty, unloading for a huge profit, when he's not
even had to lay out a cent in real terms. So I'm not so much
concerned about the why. *Who* is important.'

Even as he said it, Torrance hesitated mentally. He
glanced at Neil Bradon: the man he had pulled in from
Madison Avenue was a good advertising man, but he had
something else too, a perception that many men in higher
executive positions lacked: perception and business acumen.
He was hard, maybe even as ruthless as Paul Dorset in his
ambitions, though maybe not as committed; he was as clever
as Peter Barclay, though maybe not as sharp financially. But
he had his own qualities too. The trouble was, John Torrance
suspected now that all three of them lacked the one quality
he had always been counting upon: loyalty.

'I'm still not so certain,' Neil Bradon was insisting. 'I
would have thought that sharedealing at this stage could not be
certain of achieving a profit objective of the kind you suggest.'

'It could,' Peter Barclay announced swiftly. 'I agree with
Mr Torrance—'

'No, hold on, let me finish. We all know the EEC min-
isters are watching developments keenly. Any attempt to
really hold a financial pistol to the heads of Chevalier and
Anchédin and the others . . . that could backfire, and we, at
CADS, could be left with powder burns on our faces. And a
lower share rating. So if there has been any share-dealing—'

'There has,' Torrance broke in impatiently. 'And I want
to know how the hell it got started.'

'Pure speculation back in the States,' Dorset suggested.
'A certain amount of gambling—'

'Our company strategy must be pretty clear to anyone
who really takes the trouble,' Barclay suggested in support,
'and it wouldn't take too much to get Wall Street jumpy over
the prospects—'

'Paul.' John Torrance's voice cut across Barclay's and
Dorset raised his sleepy-lidded eyes. 'Just answer me, yes or

no: did you authorize and set up any share option proposals back in New York before we left?'

'No, sir.'

'Or since?'

'No, sir.'

'And have you given out any information to interested parties about the deals we're cooking with Anchédin and Chevalier and the others?'

'No, sir.' Paul Dorset's deep voice was passive, but certain in its force. Torrance stared at his henchman for several seconds before he turned to Peter Barclay.

'Peter, if I ask you the same questions—'

'Negative, sir. The answers are negative.'

The two Apostles declaring their faith. Torrance drew on his cigar thoughtfully, and turned to Neil Bradon. 'That leaves you, son.'

'I've done no share-dealing, sir. Not for profit, or otherwise.'

'And the information?'

'Not to interested parties, no, sir.'

John Torrance was aware of the movement of a head, a slight reaction from Peter Barclay, sharper than Paul Dorset, quick to detect a nuance in Neil Bradon's reply. Torrance was careful in his choice of question. 'No information to an interested party . . . How would you define *interest* in this context, Neil?'

A faint flush had begun to stain Bradon's features. He stared back at Torrance boldly. 'A business competitor has an interest, sir; that's the kind of interest I'm talking about.'

'Yes, I understand . . .' John Torrance was thoughtful. 'Now let's go through this slowly. The way we've set up the European operation, it's been all low key. One of the advantages of using Oakham Manor for the visit of Chevalier was that it was remote, didn't draw attention, we could keep cards close to our chests. Our cover in Paris was the EEC visit; nothing got blown there; the financial press didn't sniff us out; there's been no publicity on the merger proposals here, in Switzerland, in Brussels, in Germany. But now New

York tells me there've been *share-dealings* . . . How do you account for that, Neil?'

'I don't see that I can, sir.'

'Interested parties, you said. You gave no information to *interested* parties . . . but what about others?'

'I . . . I don't understand,' Bradon faltered.

'Think you do, boy, think you do,' Torrance said softly, his eyes glittering. 'Your words, not mine. So tell me — who did you give information about Chevalier and our strategy to? The name, Bradon, the name!'

Neil Bradon's hesitation was obvious, but it was equally clear he could not deny any longer that he had given some information away. He touched his dry lips with his tongue, and then looked up, held Torrance's cold glance. 'Miss Vallance,' he said.

Paul Dorset whistled; Peter Barclay sat up straight. John Torrance nodded slowly, thoughtfully. 'Miss Antonia Vallance . . . And just why did you do that?'

'I'm sure she wouldn't take advantage of the information,' Bradon insisted. 'It was . . . well, I felt sorry for her. She was under pressure over ownership of the estate—'

'Now resolved, it would seem,' Paul Dorset murmured.

'And she was pretty mad at our organization — still is, for that matter — and I thought it would be a good idea if I explained that CADS wasn't the great big monster she made it out to be, and how the company could actually give Oakham Manor the kind of extended life that she basically wanted for it. So I sketched in some of the background to our USA problems—'

'And you just naturally happened to bring in our company strategy,' Paul Dorset cut in.

'And told her about Chevalier's visit,' Barclay edged in spitefully, but with a hint of relief.

'Was that the way it was?' Torrance asked in a voice like steel.

After a moment, Bradon nodded. 'Something like that. I felt it important to explain to her. After all, what does she know about business? What does she know about our operation? There was no harm; she couldn't use the information—'

'*Someone* has,' Torrance disagreed. 'The information could have come from her.'

'I can't see—'

'My dear boy,' Torrance said cuttingly, 'don't be so damned naive. You talk of interested parties: *she* has an interest! Maybe it's not as clear-cut as a normal business involvement; maybe it's clouded with sentiment and emotion; maybe it's unformed — but do you really believe that if she knew the information you gave her was important she wouldn't have used it to get back at us in some way, either to stop us taking Oakham Manor, or else out of mere petty desire to strike at us the way she thinks we've struck at her and her damned manor house!'

Fiercely Neil Bradon shook his head. 'I can't believe that.'

'You'd better believe it!' Paul Dorset lumbered to his feet suddenly. 'Hell, man, you risked this whole operation just because you got sympathy for a piece of skirt, just at a time when we could be sewing things up tight! Chevalier is all but in our pocket; the Anchédin deal is hanging there like a ripe plum. We could set up the whole merger within days and you go blowing the whole thing by a bit of chat with a dame who could sell us down the river for reasons unconnected with any sense or logic in the business!'

'He's right, Neil,' Peter Barclay agreed. 'A damn stupid thing to do.'

'It still doesn't tell us who's doing the sharedealings,' John Torrance interrupted quietly. Paul Dorset stood beside him, heavy, uncompromising, angry; Barclay's face was again shadowed with a nervous uncertainty, but there was a hint of belligerent defensiveness in Neil Bradon's eyes. John Torrance walked across to the table and ground out his cigar. 'The fact is, now we've discovered who gave out the information regarding our activities, and who received it — how do we determine what use Miss Vallance put it to?'

'You're jumping to conclusions,' Bradon objected.

'Over Miss Vallance?' Dorset sneered. 'Come on, Neil, your common sense is clouded by visions of her sweetness and light. She'd do anything to save this place, and this could be one way she saw of saving it!'

Bradon shook his head. 'You're concluding she used the information, passed it on to someone else. I don't think she would have done: she didn't appreciate its significance. But in any case, who would she have passed it to? What financial contacts does she have that could damage us?'

'It only takes one stockbroker friend with any sense—' Barclay began.

'And then there's something else, you've all overlooked.'

John Torrance did not like the truculence in Neil Bradon's tone. He knew the young man was on the defensive, seeking to justify the foolish mistake he had made; Torrance knew also that there was no way Bradon could redeem this mistake, nor prove to the satisfaction of the other three men in the room that Tina Vallance could not have used the information in such a way that it led to the chain reaction of the share-dealing. At the same time, something along his back prickled suddenly: it was a feeling he had experienced several times during his business career, a feeling that always reached him at times of pressure — when that pressure had obscured true logic, a balancing of measures, a weighing of evidence that would lead to the truth.

He had come to respect that feeling; for some reason, now, Neil Bradon had brought it on again. 'So what,' he asked slowly and cautiously, 'have we all overlooked?'

'Your immediate reaction to the news that someone had been dealing in CADS shares.'

'What do you mean?'

'Your immediate reaction was to assume that one of us, in this room, had undertaken the action in the States. We, each of us, deny it — but the *guilty* party must be *expected* to deny it.'

Silkily Paul Dorset said, 'Impeccable logic, but it still doesn't explain Miss Vallance out of this situation.'

Bradon stared at him coldly for a few moments. 'Moreover, the person who really did the dealing would be more than happy to throw in this red herring about Tina Vallance. Even emphasize it.'

'Are you suggesting—'

'No more than we look at the facts!'

'And one of those facts is that you told Tina Vallance about our negotiations!'

'That's enough,' John Torrance said sharply. His glance was fixed thoughtfully upon Neil Bradon. He nodded. 'All right, I agree that all this . . . supposition gets us nowhere. The main thing is that we do something about it.'

And yet, somewhere, somehow, there was a flaw in the whole situation, a certain illogicality, a piece of the jigsaw missing. There was something they were overlooking and he concentrated for a little while, trying to make out what it was. The three young men waited silently as he stood there, staring at them blankly as the possibilities fluttered through his brain, permutations, computations, adapting the form of logical analysis he had once prided himself upon. But he had been young then, and less cynical. Now, there were considerations other than pure business which crowded in upon him, matters he would have dismissed years ago as inconsequential. Now they hovered about him, staining his mental processes, marking his old convictions about priorities until those convictions themselves became questionable.

Arnold Landon had much to answer for, the damned nonentity, and yet . . .

Savagely John Torrance shook his head. 'Whatever the truth of it is, it matters little in immediate terms. The damage is done: whether it's Tina Vallance who's responsible for the leak after Bradon behaved so stupidly, or whether it's someone else makes no difference in the long run. It's only a matter of consequences, and responsibility. Barclay?'

'Sir?'

'Set up the meeting with Chevalier, Anchédin and the others for Friday. The bleeding has to be stopped. Dorset?'

'Yes, Mr Torrance?'

'What's your schedule for the next two days?'

'I'm due to leave for London this afternoon, sir, for the royalties meetings. We're halfway towards a draft agreement and—'

Torrance waved an impatient hand. 'All right, just as long as you're available for the meeting with the others on Friday. I'll want you and Barclay there.'

'Mr Torrance.' Bradon's voice was slightly shaky. 'I'll need to know, if we're to get maximum mileage out of the Friday meeting in terms of press announcements, what the consequences of the meeting are likely to be. You'll be making an announcement of the merger arrangements with Chevalier and Anchédin on Friday, or soon thereafter?'

John Torrance glared coldly at the man who had disrupted his plans and unbalanced his thought processes by sentimental conversations with a young woman whose problems were none of Torrance's making or concern.

'On Friday,' he said bleakly, 'there will be an announcement.'

He walked stiffly out of the room, leaving a bristling silence in his wake. There was something about his attitude, and his words, that all three men still left in the room found unnerving.

CHAPTER FOUR

The rain came slanting down out of a leaden grey sky and the mist drifted along the meadow, taking all the life from the land, turning it into a silent, dark expanse where no bird sang. As the evening drew on, the sky darkened, and pools of water glittered sullenly under the reflected house lights from the Manor.

In the Red Lion, Arnold Landon reflected on what he might yet find in the passageway on the morrow.

At the motorway crash barrier fifteen miles from Oakham Manor the car lay on its roof, surrounded by flashing blue lights, the orange glow bursting from the arc lights as the oxyacetylene cutters got to work, the hollow noise of police shortwave radios echoing through the evening air. Diversion signs had already been set up, and car headlights were now lancing away from the crash area, cutting across to the other carriageway as police diverted them with waving lights, cursing as bow waves of water soaked them further under the lashing rain.

Inside the car, John Torrance heard nothing, not even the drumming of the rain on the roofs of the other cars, nor did he see the flashing of the lights. He lay still, eyes closed, his body still numb, resisting the time when the pain would begin to lance through his body. Yet strangely, for a little while, before he relapsed into unconsciousness again, he was able to remember everything that had happened, the smallest detail, the sharpest sensations. And the fear.

* * *

It had been almost five o'clock before he was able to leave Oakham Manor even though he had intended an earlier start. There had been papers to sign, some phone calls to make, and then he had learned that his chauffeur had been given the day off — after all, this was the first intimation any of them had had that he intended going up to London.

'Be easier if you leave it until tomorrow,' Neil Bradon had advised; Peter Barclay had offered to drive him up himself, even if it did mean leaving the Adilon accounts until the next day. John Torrance had rejected both their suggestions: he was not too decrepit yet to drive himself to London, and in the Porsche, he could be at his hotel in good time for dinner, and a conference thereafter.

They had looked at each other at that point and he had caught their glance: he did not tell them whom he intended meeting.

He was less than happy with the performance of the car as soon as he reached the motorway. The short drive through the lanes around Oakham Manor had not given Torrance the opportunity to open up the engine: once he left the motorway junction and slid into the fast lane he began to push the car, but it did not respond. It felt sluggish, unwilling to react to his need to achieve speed.

It was a real need, and not dictated by time. He wanted the concentration that speed would demand; he wanted the flickering lines and lights of the road to monopolize his attention; he did not want too much space to think. For his thoughts were bothersome: somewhere, he knew, he was going wrong, reading signs incorrectly, and he hoped speed would wash away sluggishness of mind, help him think clearly again. Even become certain that what he was about to do was right.

For even in that he had become indecisive. It wasn't easy, sinking with one salvo a ship he had built with his hands and mind and energy. Yet was that what he really intended to do? He could no longer be certain. The influence of the environment of Oakham Manor had affected him in a curious manner: it had stripped him of many of his certainties, made him look for new realities, listen to new concepts and viewpoints, and the process was a debilitating one. On the one hand there was Chevalier and Anchédin; on the other — what? Arnold Landon? He shook his head and the rain began to lash against the windscreen, the windscreen wipers began to beat a rhythmic pattern, and for the first time he became aware of the headlights, steady in his mirror.

It was a big car, a fast car, and the Porsche was still sluggish, unresponsive to the accelerator. After a mile Torrance gave up the struggle and moved to the centre lane; the car behind made no response, no attempt to overtake. Instead, it merely slipped into place behind the Porsche, keeping a steady distance, slowing as Torrance automatically slowed. He grunted; he knew the kind. Aware of the power that would lie in the Porsche and unwilling to try a competitive surge past, the other driver would wait for a while and then, when he became confident he could overtake without a battle, he would do so.

Torrance shrugged, and peered through the windscreen, moving steadily past the red rear lights of cars in the slow lane, manoeuvring into the outside lane when he found himself behind another car in the centre.

The headlights behind moved with him, carefully, gently, maintaining a distance.

Torrance began to get irritated; the headlights were badly aligned and bothered him so he slipped his rear-view mirror to antiglare and pressed on, speeding up as far as the Porsche would allow, but still unable to achieve more than seventy in the fast lane. He carved his way through the rain past thunderous lorries that blinded him momentarily with their spray and still the car behind kept station. He pulled in as the rain sheets lifted momentarily to give him a view of twinkling road lights a half mile ahead and he was just beginning to wonder why it was that British roadways were so unevenly lit when the car behind slipped out into the fast lane and began to edge forward.

Then it was all a nightmare.

At first, Torrance thought it was a miscalculation, as the rear of the car began to slew in towards the nose of the Porsche. The screeching of metal, obscene against the drumming of the rain persuaded him otherwise. Either the other man was drunk, or he was suicidal. Torrance dragged the wheel across, sliding the Porsche into the empty slow lane and he braked, but the wheels spun, screaming on the wet surface, and an eerie red glow filled his eyes as the car beside him braked with him, and crunched sideways into his front door. Torrance shouted, uselessly, and braked and the Porsche responded momentarily, the wheels locked and then, as the mist closed ahead of him again and visibility was severely restricted, he felt the car slide forward helplessly, aquaplaning across the smooth wet surface of the tarmac. The rest was a swift confusion as lights swung across him, there was a dark image ahead, red lights gleaming against a black tailboard, he dragged at the wheel, the nose of the Porsche touched the lorry ahead and then it was a long swinging violent parabola, the Porsche skidded crazily out of control, and with a harsh, bouncing, shuddering crash it turned over and Torrance knew he was going to die.

The engine roared and he blacked out, and then, for a little while, he was conscious again. He thought of what had happened and what was happening; he heard the silence of the car, saw the flash of headlights, heard another, distant crash. And other thoughts came crowding in: Tina Vallance, Arnold Landon, Bradon, Dorset, Barclay. And Chevalier . . . Chevalier.

And the reasons why a man called Torrance had to die.

2

If there was one thing Arnold had discovered about the landlady at the Red Lion, it was the fact of her consistency. It was more than he could say about her breakfast eggs. Interminably, they haunted his early morning hours: he still hoped they might one morning appear hard-boiled. They did not. Arnold satisfied himself with orange juice, coffee and toast. He did not dare ask for porridge. He wanted his memories of Scotland and breakfast there unsullied.

Oakham Manor seemed almost deserted when he arrived. The curtains were still drawn in the part of the manor house used by Tina Vallance, so Arnold guessed that she was either away, or disinclined to face the disappointments of the day. He could guess how she felt about the loss of Oakham Manor; in a sense it would soon be lost to him. The cataloguing was now all but complete — but there still remained the secrets of the passageway and the proving of his theory. If he was to do anything about it, the action would have to be taken quickly, for who could know what might happen once her relative Andrew Castle took over, and sold out to CADS? There had been a time when Arnold had thought that if John Torrance owned Oakham through the company it might have been a situation where further research would have been possible. Now, Torrance's disappointing lack of interest in what Arnold Landon felt and knew meant that it was, in Arnold's view, highly unlikely that he would obtain any opportunities to delve further once he — and Miss Vallance — left Oakham.

Arnold made his way down towards the old kitchens. He opened the door — silent on its oiled hinges — and stood inside on the stone-flagged floor, looking about him at the now familiar walls and vaulted beams. Yes, the buildings that still existed, they had been constructed well . . .

Tina Vallance's inheritance; now to be that of Andrew Castle. It was a pity. But there was nothing Arnold could do about that. Nevertheless, even as the thought crossed his mind, something slow and turgid moved at the edge of his conscious thought, a niggling disturbance that had touched him from time to time over the last few days. Restlessly, he walked about in the kitchens, watching the dust dance in the slanting sunlight, trying to make the errant thought steady, grow clearer in form, make its unease apparent to him in a manner he could understand and formulate.

This bille endentyd witnesseth that on the Tewesday next after the feste of Seynt Mathie Apostle the fourte yeere of Kyng Henry the Sexte . . .

It was something that touched on that blasted building contract he had discovered and discussed with the Senior Planning Officer at Morpeth. There was something about that contract which disturbed Arnold; it wasn't right; it contained an inconsistency that did not square with undisputed facts, and although his instinct warned him, his imagination and intellect failed him: he could not put his mental finger on precisely what it was that disturbed him in that ancient building contract made with *the fornsaid Richard and Adam* . . .

Arnold glared angrily about him, unseeingly, and took a deep breath. Enough of this nonsense. The more you tried to struggle with a problem, the more intractable it was likely to become. When something was stitched into the interstices of the mind, the unravelling was well-nigh impossible: it could only happen in relaxation, in swift, inconsequential thought, in the sudden, unlikely by-product of an entirely different passage of arms in the brain.

Besides, he had come down to explore the passageway.

He had armed himself appropriately, if unromantically. A shovel and a pick were his main, crude weapons; he bore also a small crowbar which he hoped would prove equal to the main task, that of loosening the brick that had been used to seal the tunnel some hundreds of years ago. He laid them aside as he applied the weight of his shoulder to the stone pillar and moved the block to expose the narrow entrance to the passageway. He took the torch from his pocket and flicked it on; the dust inside the chamber was still. Arnold picked up his tools, placed them inside the entrance, and then climbed in himself.

The chamber seemed to wrap itself around him, not comfortingly, but with a sense of the familiar and welcoming. Arnold was filled with the curious feeling that it was now taking on a life of its own, a life that had been denied it for centuries, and that meant it was ready and willing to yield up its secrets. At the same time, the fancifulness that touched him brought other, less comfortable thoughts: there was something alien in this chamber, something odd, anachronistic, that touched his senses in a way he was unable to describe, even to himself.

He shook his head, directed the beam of the torch ahead of him and scuffed his way across the dust to the far end of the chamber where it narrowed into the passageway, and where he had first discovered the brick wall that had been built to seal it off. *Latebras et diverticula* . . . Under the beam of the torch, Arnold inspected the brickwork.

It was old, decayed, corroded by dry time.

The brick had a reddish tinge unfamiliar to him, at odds with the grey, massive stone of the passage walls. The ceiling itself extended to a height of perhaps five feet and a width of four feet. It would seem that the passageway had narrowed at this point, the roof dropping to four feet, perhaps because of the configuration of the stone above or the difficulties of excavation. Wherever the passageway had anciently led, the men who had used it would have had to stoop to enter here — if the assumption that the entrance led anywhere was correct. There was the possibility that nothing lay beyond — nothing, perhaps, other than a storeroom.

He had the sudden, romantic vision of a bricked-up skeleton and he frowned, grimaced, admonished himself, and selected his point on the brickwork. It was at the edge of the stone, some three feet high: crumbled, flaking and vulnerable to the crowbar. The steel point bit deeply, the dust poured down and the brick moved under Arnold's wrenching, then suddenly collapsed, breaking away completely under the crowbar. A feeling of sadness touched Arnold: a man had built this wall centuries ago. It was almost sacrilegious to destroy it in this manner. But it was necessary if he was to discover what secrets lay beyond. He applied the steel to the next brick, and it was then that he heard the rustling sound again.

An icy finger touched his spine and his skin crawled. The fear that touched him was unreasoning and atavistic; he had an impulse to drop the crowbar and hurry away, out of the passageway and the chamber, for there was something eerie, threatening in the sound he had heard. And yet he had felt a friendliness in this darkness, an ancient reaching out from the distance of centuries. Men had worked here, men of his kind, and he knew them, appreciated their skills, and he was aware of what they had left. Yet his skin still crawled in the silence, until the rustling came again, swelled, abated, and died.

Arnold was sweating; the perspiration stung his eyes and he rubbed the back of his hand across his brow. The absurdity of his imagination took him and he shook his head: he was a grown man, fantasizing about the past and scaring himself silly because of time, and a close darkness, and overheated illusions. He applied himself again to the brickwork.

A second brick crumbled under the crowbar; Arnold inserted his fingers into the aperture and pulled at the brick until it came away. He placed it against the wall at his feet, put down the crowbar and took up the pick. He was able to place its point into the gap that had been made by removal of the two bricks: for a moment he hesitated, thinking of the destruction that had been occasioned over the years on unsupervised archaeological digs, when scant regard had been paid to history in the interests of time. He was in the same dilemma now: rough treatment was necessary, because his time at Oakham was limited, and besides, a brick wall wasn't quite the same thing as an archaeological sifting. He braced the haft of the pick and tugged, tugged again. Next moment a whole section of the brickwork collapsed towards him and he lost balance, fell backwards to collide with the wall while all around him rose a choking cloud of dust and powdery mortar.

Arnold struggled to his knees, coughing and gagging. He dropped the pick and moved back into the chamber itself, where the air was cleaner and, when his coughing had stopped, he leaned against the wall, waiting to regain his breath and watching the dust waver in the torchlight. Behind him, the faint light from the open entrance and the kitchens beyond illuminated the walls with a grey luminosity.

After some ten minutes, Arnold felt able to proceed again, his impatience heightened by curiosity and overcoming his disinclination to enter too soon into the clogged atmosphere of the passageway. The air was clearer, but still polluted; by the torchlight he could see that an aperture had now been broken into the wall, measuring perhaps some two feet in width. It would not take much effort to remove more of the brick, and make the entrance large enough for him to crawl through. He crouched at the wall, shone the torch through the hole in the brickwork and could make out stone walls again: the passageway continued, that was certain, but swung to the right in a slow curve so that he was unable to see further than a few feet. Arnold propped the torch up again and, more carefully this time, used the pick to drag away at the old brickwork, loosening individual bricks and then pulling them away one by one with his hands, to place them in a neatly stacked pile across to his right.

The atmosphere in the passageway became thicker, and Arnold was breathing hard, his shirt sticking to his back. He stopped after some ten minutes and picked up the torch, made his way back to the entrance and stepped out into the kitchens. He breathed deeply, clean air pumping into his lungs, and he looked at his hands, saw the dust and grime of them and knew he must be looking like a scarecrow. He removed his jacket and shook it. The dust rose thickly. He folded the jacket, placed it at the foot of the stone pillar, and then in a little while, cooler, breathing easily again, he made his way back into the chamber and the passageway beyond.

It took him another ten minutes to enlarge the hole in the brickwork to a size sufficient to enable him to make an entry. He stepped through, thrusting his shoulder and head into the tunnel, and then reached back to pick up the crowbar and torch. A sense of subdued excitement returned to him after the mindless effort of the previous quarter of an hour: the stone walls were partly hewn from the living rock, partly buttressed by cut blocks. It was no chamber. It was a tunnel curving ahead of him, its floor littered with broken stone and dirt, its ceiling almost six feet high at this point but rising slowly, and Arnold, head lowered, was able to move forward, the torch flickering its beam ahead of him, his left hand outflung, maintaining contact with the one wall while his shoulder brushed the other.

There were no skeletons, and here there were no whispers of danger, merely the suppressed excitement that moved in his stomach and chest, uncontrollably.

After some ten feet the tunnel straightened again and as the roof rose to some seven feet Arnold found the confidence to move more quickly, the torchlight playing ahead of him. On the roof he thought he could make out the blackening that would have been caused by rushlights and smoke emitted from torches held centuries ago, and the idea quickened his excitement. He hurried along, paying no attention to the way in which his breathing had become laboured, unconcerned about the thickness of the air, until at last he slowed, aware of the painful constriction about his temples, the dull ache that told him he was overtaxing himself in the heavy, stifling atmosphere. He stopped, leaned against the wall, and his breathing slowed in a little while, but his shirt clung to his body, heavy with sweat, and the ache, the tight band about his temples, increased throbbingly.

Arnold moved more slowly now, carefully; his legs were leaden and his hand dropped, the torchlight playing on the floor rather than the darkness ahead of him. Although he pressed on, still eager to discover where the tunnel led him, he began to be plagued by fantasies, a mixture of the past, when priests had made their secret way through this passage, and the present, when the menace of a rustling, whispering, unseen presence filled him with a vague, unaccountable panic. His lungs were straining now, gasping for oxygen in the sweating darkness, and that darkness seemed to press in upon him almost physically, beyond the narrow beam of the torch. The dust was soft under his feet and he imagined it was rising with long, gentle fingers, tendrils reaching out to touch his mouth and his throat, enter lungs, cloud his mental processes until he succumbed to its insidious pressures, kneeling to his death on the broken track the ancient monks had trod. Perhaps the warmth and the friendliness of the chamber had been a myth, a confidence-building trick practised upon him by men long since dead. Perhaps it had been merely an enticement, a leading on into a darkness from which he would never escape.

He was tired, and hot, and weary, and he stopped, knelt as he knew he should not kneel, lowered his head almost in a gesture of submission.

Nothing moved in the dust about him. He heard his breath rasping at the air, and realized what was happening to him. No single person had walked this passage for perhaps centuries and its staleness was choking him: he should dare go no further but retrace his steps to safety. And yet, he had come this far . . .

Arnold struggled to his feet. He moved onward at a laboured pace, dragging his toes in the dust, his mind tumbling with building contracts and the objectives laid down by a thirteenth-century prior, with bridges of mist and American businessmen, with the destruction of centuries and the vaulted glory of timber roofs, and suddenly he stumbled, fell forward, and was aware of rough-edged stone under his hands.

He had come up against a fall.

He lay there stupidly for several minutes, not knowing what to do. Gradually his mind began to clear, the dull ache in his temples lessened, and the throbbing in his head became less insistent. He still gripped the torch; he directed the beam forward and realized that the fall had been caused by a breaking away of the stone buttresses on the left-hand wall. The stone and rubble were piled some three feet high, blocking the passageway, but it was yet possible to crawl over the rubble and scramble through the gap between the fall and the roof above. There was at least four feet clearance, and Arnold could manage it — if he had the will.

And where, minutes earlier, he would have had neither will nor strength, he now possessed both. For there was something else. He could not be certain of it, but his senses demanded he put it to the test. He flicked off the torch and sat in the solid blackness, dragging the air into his lungs in long, slow gulps. And in a little while he became certain, as his eyes grew accustomed to the blackness and it was not black, and his lungs recognized the distinction between the heavy, dustchoked atmosphere and the hint of cool, fresh air.

He flicked on the torch again, scrambled his way over the rubble and dropped to the floor beyond. He stood upright and moved forward tentatively. Some twenty feet further on the passageway he became aware of the growing luminosity, greyness in the intense darkness, and as the tunnel curved again and the faint light grew, he stumbled forward at a faster pace and the air was lighter, easier on his lungs.

It was another fall; grey rock lay pale under a filtered light; the tunnel roof soared as the passageway opened into a natural chamber, deep under the porous hill, and high above him the narrow fissure let in light and air, in meagre quantities but sufficient to lift his heart and mind.

But there the tunnel ended.

Arnold doubted the evidence at first. The chamber was some twenty feet high, and perhaps ten feet square. He measured it, pacing around its space; he felt his way along the rough walls, solid rock, falls of dirt, and he could not understand. It would have been pointless, constructing a tunnel leading this distance from the priory, only to have it end in a blank chamber.

Centuries had passed. It was this realization that gave Arnold the answer, finally. Again he traversed the walls of the chamber, and on his second circuit he discovered what he was looking for. There *had* been an exit from this chamber, probably leading to sweet air and sky beyond. It had been sealed, more effectively than the bricked-up walling at the Manor. The walls had been brought down externally, rock thrusting into the exit, closing it completely perhaps two centuries or more ago. Arnold would never be able to break out of this confining space on his own — nor would there be any point to it. If he could find the exit from the hill itself, outside, it would be done more easily.

Nor would such a discovery be impossible. He recalled the view from his seat at Walbur: he already had a rough idea of the area in which the tunnel would be likely to emerge. All that would be required would be a careful survey of the hill, compass bearing in the tunnel, the skills of a qualified mine surveyor — it would not be difficult.

And though Arnold might never find, completely, what the purpose of the tunnel might have been — political or personal — at least his curiosity would have been satisfied. The construction of the *latebras et diverticula* rendered it unlikely that personal reasons would have been the main motivation: rather, the politics of mediaeval England might have dictated construction of the tunnel. But Arnold had little doubt that its later use, and the connection with Walbur, would have something to do with the scandals that had occurred elsewhere in monastic circles and which had probably been echoed here.

Reverberations of those scandals would have led to the closure of the tunnel, once censure had been received from the Order itself. There would have been no documentation left extant, either of the existence of the tunnel or of the reasons for its closure: the Church did not love scandal even if the laity did. All that had remained to serve as a guide would have been the words Arnold had discovered, inscribed in Latin in an ancient building instruction: *latebras et diverticula*.

It gave Arnold a thrill of pride, that from such minuscule beginnings he had been able to construct a theory and discover its evidence of existence. That, and his knowledge and understanding of a man's pride in building, and the development of patterns of construction over a span of five hundred years and more.

Arnold turned away in happier frame of mind. He would need to make only one more entry to the tunnel now, to take some survey bearings, make some notes on directions. Thereafter, at his leisure, and irrespective of what happened to the ownership of Oakham Manor, he would be able to return and work out just where the monks of old had emerged on their clandestine visits to Walbur and the charms of their sisters of the cloth. He chuckled to himself as he made his way back, wondering what the Senior Planning Officer would make of such excitements.

Inevitably, the return proved easier on his lungs, head and legs than the outward journey had been. It was the result of his satisfaction, his pride, and his knowledge now of the passageway itself. He made good progress, swifter than before, and though he still found the atmosphere heavy and thick, the thought that soon he would be standing in the kitchens again and closing the stone pillared entrance to prying eyes made him move eagerly along the dark, choking tunnel.

Until, as he neared the wall through which he had torn his way with the crowbar, his sense of unease returned. At first, it was almost imperceptible, a quickening of the pulse, an unaccountable pumping of adrenalin into his veins. He stopped, listened uneasily, then moved on again towards the broken wall, but the hairs along the back of his neck lifted damply, and he felt chilled in spite of the heaviness of the dust-laden air.

Just beyond the aperture he stopped again, and something made him lower his hand, flick out the torch. He stood there for several minutes, unable to explain to himself why he hesitated, yet dreading the thought now of stepping through the hole he had broken in the brick wall, to the chamber beyond. His heart was thumping in his chest and he listened, *concentrated* in the darkness with his eyes closed, straining for what he could not hear, yet knowing, instinctively, it was there.

When he had come into the chamber with John Torrance he had heard something and discounted it; with Tina Vallance at his side they had heard the scratching and scurrying of rats, though there had been no rats. But now there was something different again, something that was in the air, a soft, menacing sibilance — dangerous, waiting.

Slowly, quietly, with the unlit torch in his left hand, Arnold eased himself through the broken wall of brick, and stepped into the passageway beyond. He stood there again, waiting, and his skin crawled as the sibilance changed again, unformed sounds trickling through to him, cadences that were unhuman, echoes that perhaps lay only in his mind, a mind now afflicted by the close darkness that had been impenetrable for centuries, before he had broken his way into it.

It was all around him, the fear and the panic that affected his chest; his hand shook slightly and as the sounds faded he tried to pull himself together, rationalize his fears, put them aside, attribute them to an overheated imagination and the strained excitement of the last half hour.

But he did not flick on the torch as he moved slowly forward, one hand feeling its way along the stone wall, searching its way towards the wider chamber and the entrance to the kitchens beyond.

And then he froze again, terrified, as he heard the words, and the name — *Torrance* — and he knew he was not alone in the blackness of the tunnel.

Someone had entered the chamber behind him; someone was waiting there in the darkness; someone was speaking there, in a voice he had never heard before.

3

When Tina entered the room she did not see Neil Bradon immediately. He was seated in the far corner, at the small writing-table that her father had purchased in Florence so many years ago. He had several documents in front of him and was engrossed in them, so much so that he hardly seemed to notice her entrance. The result was that both of them were in the room for several seconds, unaware of the other's presence: both were suddenly startled as they saw each other.

'I'm sorry,' she said quickly. 'I didn't realize you were here. I thought you had all left—'

Neil Bradon rose to his feet. His hair was dishevelled, his tie crooked, and he seemed younger, less businesslike as a result. He waved deprecatingly towards the papers in front of him. 'I was just clearing up, really. The others have gone. I'm the last.'

'I'm sorry to have disturbed you,' she said coolly, and turned to leave the room.

'Please — don't go yet.'

She hesitated, glanced back over her shoulder at Bradon. 'I . . . I only came in to have a look around. To see the place after you'd all left it. This room was, after all, the centre of your activity at Oakham, wasn't it? Mr Torrance's nerve-centre?'

She gestured towards the two extra telephones that had been installed on Torrance's instructions before his arrival.

Neil Bradon grinned wryly. 'I suppose you can call it that. Mr Torrance spent most of his time in here — and held his meetings in this room. Carpeted us here, too.'

'Really?' Her tone suggested a lack of interest, and she moved uneasily, as though wishing to escape.

Hurriedly Bradon said, 'I'm glad you came in; I wanted to have a few words with you.'

'What about?'

'You kinda cut me off in the gardens — when I tried to say I was sorry.'

'Did I . . . and are you?'

He regarded her gravely for several seconds. 'You seem determined to prevent me from establishing any sort of bridge between us.'

'I don't see the point of building one, Mr Bradon.' Her tone was still cool, but there was a slight nervousness behind it also, as though she found the fact that they were speaking at all somewhat unsettling. 'It's not likely we would ever have found ourselves with things in common, and not least when the most important thing to me, Oakham, would inevitably be a source of dissension between us.'

He shook his head. 'Look, we got off on the wrong foot, that's all—'

'I've no objection to it staying that way.'

'I have.'

His glance was very steady and, in spite of herself, she held that glance, read the questions that lay in it. She shook her head irresolutely. 'This is silly—'

'One moment. You didn't give me the chance in the gardens. I'd heard from Castle's solicitor that negotiations between CADS and you would now be pointless since the courts had ruled in his favour. I didn't like the decision. I had hoped that it would have been settled in your favour.'

'Thank you. But as I said, it wouldn't have changed anything.'

'I think you're wrong,' he insisted. 'I'm sure you could have worked something out with CADS, to the advantage of Oakham itself. I'm sure the corporate image I would have helped build, with the help of Oakham, would have given the place a new lease of life. But I've said this before—'

'All right, I'm sorry if I bit at you in the gardens,' she said dispiritedly. 'My excuse . . . well, I'd only just then heard the news and was still trying to come to terms with losing Oakham. I wasn't inclined to talk to you or receive your sympathy. As for the rest of it . . . it's all quite pointless, now that decisions have been made. But . . . I shall miss Oakham.'

He stared at her in sympathy. 'What will you do, now?'

She managed a smile, glanced around the room and took a deep breath. 'Ah well, that's the question. Don't get me wrong: I'm not going to find myself staring in the face of penury. My father did not leave me unprovided for, even if I have had to sink more money than I would have otherwise cared into Oakham itself. No, I'll be all right for a while, until I can find a job suitable to my talents. What talents I have.' She turned away, began to walk towards the door. 'Still, I've interrupted you. No doubt you have work to complete before you hurry to join your colleagues.'

'Well, yes, in a way, but things are somewhat confused right now, with the news about John Torrance.'

She stopped inside the door, looked back at him. 'News?'

'You hadn't heard?'

'I've been somewhat . . . withdrawn these last twenty-four hours. A sort of process of self-immolation would be one way to describe it. So what's happened, in respect of Mr Torrance?'

'He's been involved in an accident. On the motorway. No one seems to be able to piece together quite what happened, but it was raining, there was a lorry involved, and just maybe another car, though they haven't been able to trace it or its driver—'

'Was Mr Torrance hurt?'

'He spun off the road. It seems he's badly hurt. He's still alive, and they're not letting him see anyone at the hospital—'

'Not even family?'

'He has no family,' Bradon said shortly.

'Oh . . . I'm sorry he's been hurt . . . I quite liked him, in a funny sort of way, in spite of the fact he was likely to take Oakham from me. Odd, isn't it, how you can like someone whom you see as an enemy?'

'But not impossible, I hope.'

The steadiness of the words, and their obvious inference, brought back to her the memory of that moment in London, outside the Wig and Pen, when her anger had been mixed with a curious breathlessness and excitement. She shrugged, uneasily. 'Let's just say it's difficult.'

'But not *impossible*,' he insisted.

She was suddenly reluctant to leave the room; at the same time she did not want to pursue the direction in which the conversation was taking them. Hurriedly she said, 'I hope he does recover, anyway, and quickly. I imagine you and your colleagues do too. You said things are now somewhat . . . confused? Because of Mr Torrance's accident?'

He nodded slowly. His eyes were suddenly careful, watchful, and she got the impression he was weighing something in his mind before he spoke. His tone was surprisingly careless when he did speak again. 'Confused is the word. You'll know we had some big deals brewing; no one can be quite sure how they'll turn out now.'

'How do you mean?'

'Well, John Torrance was pretty central to them: they demanded his presence, his control. Now he's ill—'

'He'll have someone to deputize for him, surely?'

Neil Bradon scratched his cheek. 'That's a moot point. The structure of CADS isn't quite as simple as that. The Apostles—'

'By that you mean Mr Barclay and Mr Dorset, I imagine.'

'Right. Those two have been groomed to play central roles in the organization and management of the company, roles which are supportive and carry a great deal of power.'

'And you?'

'Third tier stuff,' Bradon said deprecatingly, but she felt his dismissiveness was a shade too facile. 'The problem for CADS is that Torrance has always held the reins so firmly himself that it's never been clear which of his two lieutenants would eventually succeed him.'

'One of them would be bound to?'

'Knowledge is power. Only those two have enough knowledge of CADS's total enterprise to control it. They have the confidence of the banks, and that's where the key lies. Finance. So, yes, one of them will succeed him.'

'So there's likely to be the beginnings of a power struggle for company control now Mr Torrance is ill in hospital?'

Neil Bradon smiled sardonically. 'Not the beginnings of one. It's been going on for years. Those two characters, they hate each other's guts, but both keep their feelings cloaked in Torrance's presence. He knows well enough, even so, that they'd tear at each other once he's out of the way. It would have been his intention to prevent that, when the time came to hand over the reins, by building one up, making him the heir apparent.'

'It hasn't happened yet?'

Bradon shook his head. 'Mr Torrance wasn't ready yet to contemplate a handover. He's an old man, and old men cling to power as long as they can.'

'But now . . .'

'Now is crunch time, seems to me.' Bradon hesitated, then said quietly, 'It will make quite a difference to shareholdings, of course, this accident to Mr Torrance.'

'In what way?'

Bradon walked away from the table towards her, casually. 'Well, you've got to appreciate, when a man like Torrance builds a big business like CADS and runs it for thirty years, inevitably the well-being of the company comes to be associated with the health of the man himself. If Torrance is near death, a lot of confidence will ooze from the people backing the company — at least until another strong man is seen to take his place.'

'And this lack of confidence will have an impact upon share prices. Yes, I see that.'

She was aware of his scrutiny as he said, 'That's right. So anyone who's holding CADS shares right now could suffer financially. And anyone who's been *gambling* in buying such shares, well, he could catch a real financial cold.'

Tina Vallance was no fool. She could detect an undercurrent in his tone that should be holding some meaning for her. She did not understand what he was driving at, but in some way she was being tested. Her hand was still on the door; slowly, she closed the door and stood facing him, her back against the woodwork. 'There has been some . . . trading in CADS shares recently?'

'Some.'

'You endow that word with a certain significance.'

'Do I?' Neil Bradon's eyes were suddenly hooded, and there was a certain tension apparent in the way he held himself, the way he moved. 'I told you a little while ago that this room was where John Torrance operated from — and where he carpeted us.'

'What reason would he have for . . . carpeting you?'

'You remember . . . in the garden, when you wouldn't speak to me? John Torrance called a meeting after that — me, Paul Dorset, Peter Barclay, the three closest to him, the three who know most about the day-to-day operation of the business.'

'A carpeting?'

'That's right. And I ended up as the one who — to mix the metaphor — got the rug pulled out from under me.'

'How?'

'I was accused of leaking information about the company to a person who might use it to the disadvantage of the operation dear to CADS's heart.'

She stared at him for several seconds, her eyes steady on his. At last, quietly, she said, 'You're talking about the merger proposals that your company is presently involved in.'

'Right.'

'And the leaking of information . . .' She hesitated. 'It was to me.'

'Right again.'

'So—'

He shrugged, his mouth twisting in an unpleasant grimace as though he disliked himself for using the words that came necessarily to his lips. 'So the question is, did you put what I told you to any practical use?'

'What kind of use are you—'

'Aw, come on, Tina!' he snapped with a sudden flash of anger that was directed as much towards himself as her. 'You're not naive; you know what I'm driving at. I've talked about share movements. Torrance suggested to me that I was unwise in talking to you about the European merger operation. I told him you had no interest in the business deal; his reaction was to point out that there are many ways of defining an *interest*. Yours is, in the main, the preservation of Oakham and the way of life you want to see retained here. How far will you go to maintain that ideal? I don't know; you won't let me get close enough to you to find out. But Torrance and the others, they're not bemused by what might be happening between you and me, not confused by the kind of problem we might be facing. And to that extent they think more logically and clearly.'

Her breathing was almost painful; there was a tight, angry, excited band about her chest. 'Where does their logic take them?'

'They wanted to know whether you would have used the information I gave you to attain your own ends — the retention of Oakham. They wanted to know whether I thought you would have contacted a stockbroker, started some share-dealings to buy into CADS and use the insider information you'd managed to get. You could have made a killing on that deal.'

'*If* I'd done it.'

'And you could also have damaged, perhaps irrevocably, the standing of CADS in the European field of operations.

Because the EEC would hold back; they'd see a rip-off which CADS couldn't explain; they'd squeal because of the damage done to European firms. And all that could have meant the destruction of the link with Chevalier, the merger, the withdrawal from Europe and the end of Torrance's dream. All the result of a sympathetic chat in a London pub; all because I felt sorry for you, and understood the nature of your feelings about Oakham.'

Her chin was up defiantly; she knew there would be the hint of tears in her eyes; she could no more explain them than she could the thudding of her heart — angry, disturbed, proud, defiant. 'I have some questions to ask of you,' she said.

He took a deep, angry breath, but she knew the anger was directed as much towards himself as her. 'Such as?'

'First: you said I *could* have made a killing, on any share-dealing as a result of the information you gave me.'

'You've a sharp ear for nuances,' he said, grumbling. 'That's right — *could* have. The matter is of academic interest only now. Those share-dealings would have made problems for us at CADS with the European connection, but in the short term the movement would have been upwards, once the news of a merger with Chevalier and Anchédin broke on the market. Your friends . . . you . . . whoever, could have got out early with quite a slice of money, before the crash came when EEC refused to back the merger and Chevalier and Anchédin pulled out. But now . . .'

'The accident to Mr Torrance—'

'Right. Different complexion on everything. He's in hospital; share prices will slide anyway; by the time they're bottoming out, a new arrangement could well be operating. It all depends now upon who emerges as the leader in Torrance's absence, and how forceful he is in projecting the merger. So, yes, an academic question. Now, your information could have little effect upon the situation, if you used it as Torrance suggested you might have done.'

She braced her back against the door; her hand, still gripping the door handle, was now damp and sticky. 'The

141

second question is a simple one. You are asking a question of me in all this: you want to know whether or not I *did* use the information you gave me to strike at CADS for my own ends. My question is: do you believe I used it?'

He made an angry, dismissive gesture with his right hand, and shook his head. 'There have been times . . .' He shook his head again. 'No, Tina; I don't believe it. There's been share-dealing, but I can't believe it arose as the result of my talking to you. I don't believe you had anything to do with it; I don't believe you used that information as John Torrance suggested you might have done.'

There was a short silence between them. Neil Bradon was unable to meet her eyes, and in a way she was glad for that, since she feared he might see something she was yet unwilling to admit to. They stood there facing each other, Bradon uncharacteristically nervous, Tina still braced against the door, unwilling to let him become aware of the weakness in her legs.

'Is that all?' he asked, at last.

'No. One more question.' He looked at her then, as she spoke, maybe because he caught something of her weakness in the tone of her voice. 'Was it . . .'

'Yes?'

'*Is* it important to you that I should confirm what you believe?'

He laughed; it held an echo of the trembling that was affecting her whole body. 'We've hardly touched, Tina; and our conversations have been only this side of hostile. What's happening to us?'

Yet the question was superfluous; they both knew precisely what was happening to them.

* * *

When the silence returned it was deep and soft and gentle while the darkness itself was like a benediction. There was about it an ancient reassurance, a confirmation that it was the harshness of the present that had been the disturbing influence among the dust and the confining, embracing darkness.

His pulse was slow and patient; his mind no longer racing with fear. He slid down with his back against the centuries-old stone and sat with the blackness about him; it gave him opportunity to think without distraction, chance to envisage with a new clarity the sounds, the smells, the sights that had greeted him here the first time, and the second, and the third . . .

In such a blackness, the senses became sharpened, and he could recall the alienations he had perceived and yet not recognized, the differences, the anachronisms that he should, with all his experience and pride in *feeling* for the past have seized upon at once. He had not then; he did so now.

In a little while he flicked on the torch, rose, and investigated the far corner of the chamber. The dark patch there had dried now, black under the light of the torch beam. He sniffed at the stale air and almost imagined he could detect that odour he had been aware of earlier, but it was probably imagination. No matter; there was a vast feeling of satisfaction in his chest now. It was not due to his unravelling of a skein of problems for there was much yet that puzzled him and required explanation. Rather, it was the result of an appreciation that Oakham had not failed him, that a betrayal had not been a betrayal, and that he, of all the inconsequential mortals in the world, still had answers to give and solutions to present.

Even to Detective Inspector Carter.

CHAPTER FIVE

1

It was one of the paradoxes observable in human behaviour, Arnold Landon had long ago concluded, that certain individuals who were accorded a relatively lowly status in life nevertheless were capable of, and seen to be wielding, the most powerful influence in social situations. The nanny, he understood, though not from personal observation, was one such individual: a power far removed from the person's social status. In a different sphere, the lawyer: a man who had little understanding of or experience in human relationships was nevertheless regarded as the appropriate individual to put forward an explanation, not least in human mitigation terms, of personal behaviour.

Another was the matron.

Arnold was terrified of hospital matrons. They far transcended, in his imagination and belief, the godly status of the surgeon: they were endowed with superhuman percipience, an unmatchable power, a *presence* that was undilutedly immense, and if he were forced to admit it the individual matron who now stood before him, Junoesque in build and Jovial in muscular heartiness, could be seen only as the essence of the species, the example to prove the rule. She frightened him to death, with her forearms, her biceps, her calm and her power, her thin lips, ice-blue eyes, and massive, Zeppelin-like bosom.

'He's prepared to *see* you,' she announced and imbued the statement with cataclysmic disapproval.

Arnold had already been treated to a harangue of considerable depth and feeling concerning the necessity to treat patients with disdain, indifference to personal desires, and firm-handedness. He was now suffering from the defeat of such objective reaction: the wishes of the matron had been overruled; money, personal presence, age and insistence had overcome her own personal discipline and she had been told in no uncertain terms that she should do as she was told. It had taken an eminent surgeon and a hesitant houseman who was on the point of leaving, to do so, but she had now finally succumbed.

'I do not approve,' she announced to Arnold as he fluttered at the entrance to the private room.

Burdened with her disapproval, Arnold edged his way into the room and stood quietly near the door, observing the elderly man who lay in the bed.

He was observed in his turn.

'You are surprised, Mr Landon.'

'They told me you were receiving no visitors.'

'They were right. But . . .' The old man in the bed moved gently, uneasy at the thought that his body was no longer receptive to his mind's signals, and sighed. 'Well, I am tired. And tiredness in a man my age is a danger. I do not wish to be bothered by young, bustling executives; the sycophancy of a second-in-command is the last reality I want to be faced with; walls here are pale and quiet and give me neither physical nor mental stimulation, and I could die here and who would really care? There would be a flurry on the stock market, sure — but is that the only feeling a man wants to leave behind?'

Arnold shifted hesitantly from one foot to another. 'That hardly explains why you are prepared to see me, when you turn away your own colleagues, your own company—'

'Henchmen. Yes. But then, you are different, aren't you, Mr Landon?'

It could have been the Senior Planning Officer speaking. 'I'm not sure—' Arnold began.

'Of course you're sure. You're the only man who *knows* unerringly he's different,' John Torrance insisted. 'That's why you're here, and the others are not. You're so damn different, you're the only man I can learn from. Because me, I'm the spawn of the business world and there are a million like me. Not you; you're an individual. I lost my individuality fifty years ago, and maybe more.'

'Mr Torrance—'

'No. Let me say it. Success is not about outward trappings; it's about a vision of oneself. And how many of us can in the end be satisfied by an internal vision? You can. You *know* who you are: you've worked at the understanding. Maybe your father gave it to you. Mine didn't. And I'll never know. So which of us is the real man?'

In spite of himself, Arnold was moved. 'Mr Torrance, that can't be right. You have all the trappings—'

'That's the word. Trappings. But after a lifetime of endeavour and success, in material terms, what are you left with? A hospital bed; a realization that you *feel* little; and the acceptance that somewhere along the line you've missed out. But you don't know on what. So do you know why you're here and the others aren't, Mr Landon?'

'No, sir.'

'Because I need to learn from you, the way I learned that morning, that day when you talked to me about irrelevant things, matters dead and gone, buildings and timber and stone; but things you believed in. I believe in little, Mr Landon.'

'People.'

'Maybe.'

'I have nothing to teach you, Mr Torrance.'

John Torrance's face was marked with a faded humour. His eyes were hollowed; the skin of his cheeks was tinged with a greyness Arnold had not noted before. Torrance was suddenly old in a way he had not been earlier: disillusion marked his features. 'Teach me? You already did, and I wasn't capable of listening. You remember that time we talked. I *slavered* over what you had to say, my friend. And when, together, we found that passageway, that chamber — I was a child again, with all the excitement and passion and freedom of childhood. Until, well, until I became a man again, an old husk of a man who lacked imagination and excitement and had merely to face his responsibilities . . .' Torrance paused, mused for a few moments. 'And yet, not quite . . .' He moved painfully in his hospital bed. 'You made me think, Mr Landon, and you made me take decisions . . .'

'I can't believe I am responsible for that kind of reaction,' Arnold said. 'But if it's true . . . Anyway, no matter, I thought I should come to see you—'

'You saw it as a betrayal, didn't you?' John Torrance asked.

It would have been less than honest to deny it. Arnold shrugged. 'Not so much the . . . failure to come back. The telling of others . . . that, well, yes, I saw that as a betrayal.'

A spasm of pain crossed John Torrance's features as he moved again in the bed. 'I didn't tell anyone else about the discovery. It was ours.'

Arnold stared at him. After a few seconds, he nodded. 'I believe that. Now.'

John Torrance's body was hurt but his mind was still active. His eyes gleamed as he caught the nuances that lay behind Arnold Landon's tone. 'You've something to tell me, about that passageway.'

'A great deal. But first . . . you told no one about our discovery? There was no betrayal?'

'Only for myself,' Torrance grunted. 'I *enjoyed* your company, and that scared me. Power . . . it corrupts in most unusual ways. However, what are you about to tell me?'

'I've been into the chamber again, and the passageway. I broke through a wall at the back; it led to a tunnel. I followed it; it's ancient. And I believe, for various reasons, that I know what it was for. Originally, maybe, an escape route in troubled political times. Later, a clandestine passageway to assuage the torments of the flesh—'

'You fascinate me!'

'The priory . . . and the nunnery. Such scandals were not uncommon.'

John Torrance lay back on his pillows, smiling slightly, breathless. His eyes twinkled above the pain as he watched Arnold Landon. 'I have the feeling you have more than this to tell me.'

'Not of such historical matters. They've faded in my mind. There are other matters, much closer in time, and of more importance to you, I suspect. I know about Chevalier, and about Anchédin, and now, about other things, too.'

'*The devil you do*,' John Torrance murmured, and closed his eyes. In the long silence that followed Arnold was faced with the real possibility that John Torrance had died. He did not want it to be so; and after a while Torrance opened his eyes.

'You're conning me, my friend,' Torrance announced in a mildly reproving tone. 'You know the names, but you don't know the consequences.'

'True,' Arnold admitted.

'But you're aware of the importance they might attach to my activities in CADS,' Torrance murmured, and again shifted painfully in the bed. 'So I have to ask the question: how did you come to hear these names?'

'They came to me, out of the darkness,' Arnold replied. 'I was in the tunnel,' he added, and John Torrance sighed and closed his eyes again.

* * *

In a little while, Arnold explained. He told John Torrance about his journey into the depths of the passageway that he and Torrance had discovered together; he went on to explain how tired and shaken he had been, how his mind had seemed to play tricks with him. He told Torrance how it had been when he had returned to the chamber, felt fear take him by the throat, pump adrenalin into his veins, weaken his powers of concentration and rationalization.

'It was the sibilant sounds, the whispers, and the rustling.'

John Torrance moved uneasily, wincing as pain took him. 'That first time, when I was down there, I *thought* I heard something. I put it down to imagination, the effect of being in that ancient chamber.'

Arnold nodded. 'It was the same for me, too. When we were together that day, I said nothing. And much the same situation occurred later, when I took Tina Vallance to the tunnel.'

'You showed it to her?'

'There seemed to be no reason not to show her. She already knew of its existence, in fact. Neil Bradon told her that we'd discovered a tunnel—'

'Bradon!'

'That's right. You'll remember, the day we were rooting around down there in the kitchens. Bradon had spoken to us, asked you some question or other in the courtyard. It's possible he got curious about why we were down there so long; maybe he checked later, found the entrance, I don't know. I have a feeling he never actually *inspected* the tunnel, and attached little importance to it, or he wouldn't have told Tina about it.'

'And you showed it to her.'

'I thought you'd already broken our agreement. It's clear now we *had* no secret really. Anyway, the point is, when I was down there with her she heard the same as I. We thought it was the scratching of rats and we got out rather hastily. But it wasn't rats.'

'Tell me.'

'The scratching of pen on paper; the scraping of a shoe; the rustle of a dress; the murmur of a conversation; you name

151

it, Mr Torrance. But the fact is, every sound, *every slightest sound* in that chamber has a root in reality.'

'I don't understand.'

'We once talked . . . you said you thought the mediaeval masons built well. They did, and some built according to specifications. There's no way of telling until we can have a really close look at it all, so I don't know whether it was a deliberate device, but the fact is there's a crevice, a narrow stone channel in that roof which acts as a perfect sounding device. It's like a narrow chimney in construction; I don't know whether it was deliberately built or not. My guess is that the tunnel was certainly used, clandestinely, for visits to the nunnery on the hill at Walbur. But at some time that channel was built, or discovered and perhaps enlarged, with the deliberate intention of using it as a listening device.'

'And—'

'The result was,' Arnold said, 'every word that has ever been uttered in one of the rooms at Oakham Manor has funnelled down to that chamber!'

The old man weighed the words he had heard. 'You say *one* of the rooms.'

Arnold nodded. 'That's right. It's impossible now to tell what the original purpose of the chamber and the listening system might have been. Perhaps the room to which it was connected was the prior's; maybe that room was the one in which issues political to the priory were discussed. Or maybe it was the prior's private chapel — and when he could be heard at his devotions, others would know it was safe to leave the priory by the passageway, to head for the nunnery on the hill at Walbur. But no matter: the fact is that the crevice provides a perfect listening device, and picks up the slightest sound. The sound is somewhat distorted, certainly, but every word said is understandable. It's where I heard the names Chevalier and Anchédin.'

'Who used them?'

'Neil Bradon. He was talking to Miss Vallance.'

'I'd had suspicions—'

'So I gathered,' Arnold interrupted. 'They're unfounded. Miss Vallance didn't use the information; Bradon was just checking on it when I overheard their conversation.'

John Torrance stared at the ceiling thoughtfully. He grimaced. 'Ah well, it makes little difference, anyway.'

'I wouldn't know about that. I thought you not only would like to know about the sounding device; I thought you *ought* to know about it.'

'Why?'

'Because the room to which it is connected, the room in which I overheard Bradon talk to Miss Vallance, is the room which you used as — Bradon's words — the nerve-centre of your operations during your stay at Oakham Manor.'

Torrance's glance slipped to Arnold and held him coldly. 'You're telling me that every conversation I held in that room was capable of being overheard in the chamber?'

'That's right.'

The silence grew about them, lengthened, and Arnold stared at his hands. At last John Torrance said, almost whispering, 'Tell me.'

Uneasily Arnold replied, 'I can't be certain now, but the first hint . . . the first thought I had that you'd betrayed your promise about keeping the chamber secret, it was the very next time I entered it. There was something different about the place, something anachronistic, but I couldn't place it at all.'

'You can now?'

Arnold nodded. 'Cigarette smoke. I'm a non-smoker, and so my sense of smell is particularly offended . . . Someone had been in the chamber, and had smoked a cigarette.'

'Who?' Torrance asked harshly.

'And then there was something else. I found this on the floor.' Arnold held up the small piece of tinfoil he had discovered in the chamber so that the old man could inspect it. A spasm of irritation crossed John Torrance's face. 'So?' he demanded.

'I'm not certain what it is, or what it's from,' Arnold admitted. 'But it *could* be part of the covering of tape—'

153

'Sticky tape?'

'Electronic,' Arnold suggested.

John Torrance stared at him, puzzled. 'You're suggesting—'

'There is the possibility that someone else found out about the chamber. He discovered, before I did, just how it operated as a listening-post. Every word you uttered, every phone call you made in that room above, could be heard down there — and *recorded*, if need be.'

'But why recorded?'

'Perhaps because the discoverer wouldn't want to be the one who actually *listened* down there. Maybe he'd have other things to do.'

John Torrance was silent for a little while.

His mouth twisted unpleasantly. 'I can imagine — like be in the room with me, when called.'

'How do you mean?'

Torrance glared at Arnold. 'I told no one about the chamber. But my aides are curious men. It will have puzzled them, my postponing the trip to Paris merely to talk with you. It would certainly have been in character for at least one of them — if not all three — to try to retrace my steps. And any one of them — Bradon, Dorset or Bradley — could have found the chamber.'

Quietly Arnold said, 'But there would surely have been little point in recording information to which, as your aides, they were already privy.'

'But what if I hadn't told them what I intended to do?' John Torrance asked fiercely.

'Was that the case?'

John Torrance sighed and stared at the ceiling again. 'Ah, it all seems so pointless now I'm lying here in my bed. I can't recall much about the crash, you know. I seem to recall a car . . . but the brain protects itself, doesn't it . . . ? Covers up unpleasant things by forgetfulness. Still . . . the fact is, Mr Landon, I haven't been entirely honest with my aides.'

'For good reason, I'm sure.'

'I'm *not* so sure. But it was your influence, anyway.'

'My influence?'

'That's right. You introduced me to *Grisild the Second*.'

'I'm afraid I don't understand . . .'

'You've got to appreciate what it's been like all these years. Business has been my life, and the business I finally built was the result of a great deal of personal labours. But the crazy thing about business is, the more successful you become, the less it really impinges upon your heart and mind. You *think* things haven't changed; you believe you're driving for the same goals; but then there's a time when the little niggling doubts at the back of your mind flower and you recognize the truth. You see, Mr Landon, that's what happened to me when I read that piece from *Grisild*.'

'Why?'

'The niggles came to the surface. I took stock of myself and my situation. And I didn't like what I saw. These last few years in the States, they've been hard. We'd reached an optimum size, I know that now, but push and ambition, the mindless kind, kept CADS grabbing on. Till we hit US legislative problems. The answer? Europe! So back I leapt on to the treadmill. It was a whole new wheeler-deal to start: negotiations with Chevalier, Anchédin and the others. But it was all being done without heart — and Chevalier knew it — and it was all being done without a sense of purpose on my part. A mechanical exercise that hadn't been weighed and measured in the manner I would have done in the old days.'

'And the book brought you up short?'

'*Most cunning workmen*.' John Torrance moved his hands in assent. 'That's right. Because as I thought about it, I knew I could apply the strictures in that passage to my own organization. It's like every system: once it gets too big, outgrows itself, corruption sneaks in. The time-savers, the flatterers, the "experts" you don't need, the advisers who tell you what you want, not need, to hear. A vast bureaucracy builds up, productivity disappears as fast as imagination, and the tracks you laid as a young, thrusting company get covered by the leaves of time schedules, corporate strategies, budget analyses and all the paraphernalia without which a large inefficient organization cannot rationalize its existence. I realized that for years I'd been carrying other men's dreams, not my own, feeding other men's egos — and at cost to the business I myself had built. And I decided, one night at Oakham Manor, that it had to stop.'

'What decision did you take?' Arnold asked curiously.

Torrance smiled thinly. 'I decided to bring a halt to the whole thing. I phoned a couple of people in New York to discuss the details. In short, I decided to stop the European merger, and cut back CADS, fine it down to a smooth, honed machine again, stripping away the unnecessary glamour, the hangers-on, the foolish dreams. That was all. A simple decision — but one that would rock the company, all the way back to Boston.'

'Your senior executives—'

'Wouldn't have liked it. They'd have balked, tried to stall it, stop it. So I had to take the step without their knowing; that's why I phoned late at night—'

'From the room in which every word of yours could be heard — and was possibly being recorded.'

John Torrance's eyes glittered. 'I made a fuss when I heard there'd been dealings in CADS shares, because I thought there'd be trouble in Europe, whether or not I was going to stop the merger. But now you've told me this . . . it makes a big difference.'

'I don't understand.'

'It makes the whole thing more serious. The dealing must have been the work of one of the senior executives. There'd be one reason for it. He knew I was about to cut back CADS activity; there was one way he could stop it. By building up a big enough shareholding to get me removed from the chair of CADS. It can be done: my own holding is only twenty-eight per cent — it's been enough in the past. Now . . . You see what I mean, Mr Landon? Whoever listened down in that chamber set up the share deals — so it follows that if you can find out for me who's behind the share-dealings, you'll also be able to tell me who's out to stop me fining down the CADS operation.'

'Me?'

'I can trust you,' Torrance said fiercely. Arnold Landon stared at him thoughtfully.

'That may be so, but there's something else.'

'Such as?'

'Your injuries. They might not have been . . . accidental.'

'You're crazy—' John Torrance began, and then a spasm touched his mouth. He frowned and glanced angrily at Arnold as though he had caught a swift glimpse of a moment in past time. 'Not accidental . . . What reason would you have—'

'You were on your way to finalize the destruction of the merger proposals, weren't you? Could that be allowed, by a ruthless man?'

'That's some ruthlessness! You can't be serious—'

'I'm not sure,' Arnold said. 'But if there *was* someone down in that chamber recording your conversation it would not have been the executive you fear. It was someone else.'

'Who?'

'A man who told me he was an electronic engineer.'

John Torrance stared at him. 'You're talking about—'

'A man called Enright. He was found some miles away, but there are bloodstains in that chamber, someone had been smoking down there, and the tinfoil wrapping . . . The thing is, why was Enright murdered? Maybe because he was of no further use? Isn't that the kind of ruthless calculation that can also lead to a car accident, when the stakes are so high?'

* * *

Suffering from the injuries he had received in the car crash, John Torrance might have been forgiven for lapsing into weakness and lack of concentration. Instead, Arnold found himself admiring the old man's strength of purpose; his

157

determination seemed to grow as the minutes ticked past. Before Arnold's arrival he had been withdrawn. When Arnold arrived pain had been uppermost, but as the story of the chamber had unfolded and its ramifications became apparent, Torrance seemed to have gained in strength.

'It will be one of the three.'

'Bradon?'

'Or Barclay, or Dorset.' Torrance grimaced. 'They're all rivals, you know: each sees himself as my natural successor.'

'Even Neil Bradon?'

Torrance's brow clouded momentarily. 'I'm not sure. He has the ability . . . indeed, at one time, but for that slip with the Vallance girl . . . The fact is, I never made it clear which one I favoured. A man can sour in such a climate, I realize that now.'

'You didn't tell any one of them about the chamber?'

'No. But we know Bradon knew of its existence; curiosity might have drawn him there after we left. But there was Barclay too: it was from him I got the blasted torch, to light our way into the tunnel. As for Dorset, he may appear sleepy at times, and unconcerned, but he watches Peter Barclay like a hawk, and isn't a man to underestimate.' He was silent for a while, and then when he looked towards Arnold his eyes were glittering. 'It all comes down to you, Mr Landon.'

'Me?'

'I have a remarkable respect for you, because you've shown me much, taught me much in a very short space of time. Now, I want you to act on my behalf.'

Confused, Arnold waved his hands helplessly. 'I don't understand—'

'I can't trust any of my three aides. But I do trust you. This Enright business, it's for that Detective Inspector Carter to sort out. My accident . . . well, we can't be certain, can we? The mind plays funny tricks . . . But the rest . . .'

'You mean the company?'

'I had decided upon a course of action,' John Torrance said slowly. 'It may be I'm lying here because someone tried to stop me doing what I intended. And all of it, the wheeling and dealing, the recordings in the tunnel, they've all led up to this. And I'm here, helpless. I *need* someone, Mr Landon; someone I can trust, someone who understands what I *feel*.'

'To do what?' Arnold asked helplessly.

'To act on my behalf, as my representative, at the merger meeting on Friday.'

2

The room was full of light. The windows curved gently along the length of one wall, the curtains drawn back to allow maximum advantage of the view of the river, with the Tower and St Katharine Docks in the distance. Nervously Arnold had stared at that view for several minutes, watching the boats slipping in and out of the lock to the marina in the dock, observing the thronging of colour, tourists milling about the entrance to the Tower. His mind had been far away, however, as he still struggled with the question why he was here at all, thrust into an important business meeting where millions of dollars could be at stake, where European finance was to be tossed around the table, where decisions of great moment would be taken, and where one of the men present might be a murderer.

'Mr Torrance,' he had protested, 'I'd be out of my depth. I've no experience—'

'You've greater experience than you believe; of men; of motives; of realities. You've taught me a great deal. You opened my eyes. You're an outsider. You're a man who — relies on his instincts. Instinct is something that gets dulled with time; a businessman can lose it: statistics, figures, profit-and-loss accounts, they can dull your senses, put you out of touch with realities, with the cunning workmen you employ. You can lose your *imagination*. You haven't.'

'But—'

'I want you to go there. Do what I want. But equally, follow your instincts; do what you think is *right*.'

'I'm not at all sure, Mr Torrance,' Arnold had remonstrated, unhappily.

'But there's still one more thing. Before I set out in the Porsche I'd put in several phone calls to New York and Boston. I faced up my aides and they each denied having undertaken the share deals. I let it go, and set up the Friday meeting, but I also instructed my agents in New York and Boston to make certain inquiries. The answers will be channelled back to London. My agents there are called Bewley and Scott. They're stockbrokers. They will be able to tell me who did the share-dealing in the States. By the time you go into that meeting on Friday you'll have that information. Make what use of it you deem fit.'

But it had not worked out that way. Arnold had contacted Bewley and Scott; they told him they had received the instruction from Mr Torrance, but the information had not yet come through from New York. They would let him have it as soon as it arrived.

But in a matter of minutes the meeting would begin, and Arnold would face one of the most frightening experiences in his life.

What on earth would the Senior Planning Officer think of it all?

* * *

They came in one by one, to take their seats at the gleaming mahogany table arrayed with leather writing-pads, gilt pens and neatly printed nameplates. Arnold had read the nameplates and watched as each man entered:

Paul Dorset, heavy, a frown on his face betraying a certain tension, and quickly behind him, Peter Barclay, his narrow eyes suddenly uncertain as he caught sight of Arnold seated at the end of the table with no nameplate in front of him. A third man came in and sat a little apart from the two Apostles: his face was vaguely familiar with its sagging cheeks and confident eyes, but he too had no nameplate. Andre Chevalier seated himself to the left of the chair. Arnold admired the measured calm of his features and the sharp clarity of his glance which dwelled thoughtfully on Arnold for a little while before dismissing him. The chair was taken by Sir Charles Fredericks.

Arnold had heard of Fredericks. A Euro MP, he was known to hold considerable stakes in the Swiss firm of Anchédin and to be a man of considerable wealth and of even more considerable business reputation. He had been criticized from time to time for the use he was alleged to make of his political European connections, but his supporters strongly emphasized his integrity and demanded that detractors produce evidence of financial misdemeanours: to date, no one had done so. He had a perfect politician's face: lean-cheeked, somewhat ascetic, silver-winged dark hair, and a fine mouth that could put an antagonist into a defensive position and a friend at ease. He had lost his wife the previous year and his cool eyes held hints of damage at the grief. He was reputed to be a man of balance and control, emotionally, politically and professionally.

He would be taking the chair because of the interest the EEC were taking in the merger proposals, and because of the absence of John Torrance.

Typically, it was the first remark Fredericks made. He glanced around the table, and announced, 'You will all no doubt be aware that Mr Torrance cannot be with us today, as a result of the unfortunate car accident two days ago. I am sure we are of one mind in hoping that he recovers from his injuries swiftly and completely.'

There was a murmur of assent; Arnold inadvertently glanced towards Dorset and Barclay, but the eyes of both men were lowered to the table.

'It is normal,' Fredericks was continuing, 'to have an assembly of secretaries at meetings of this nature, but I thought best that we should decide first whether members might wish to dispense with such support in view of the nature, importance and . . . ah . . . necessary secrecy which must surround our decisions. Are we in agreement?'

There was a murmur of assent.

'The lack of such formality, of course,' Fredericks went on, 'means I am not completely informed regarding all present. Mr Dorset and Mr Barclay, you represent CADS, of course; M'sieur Chevalier is well known to me, and I am able to speak for Anchédin, but . . .'

His eyes dwelled on the man with the sagging face. It was Paul Dorset who spoke, however. 'May I introduce Mr Andrew McNeil Castle, Sir Charles? He has been involved with CADS recently in the negotiation over Oakham Manor, and this is likely to lead to certain share purchases. He has asked that he might be present as an observer, under my sponsorship.'

That Sir Charles thought the necessity for Castle's presence a flimsy one was clear from the long silence that followed Dorset's remark, but then he shrugged slightly and turned his glance in Arnold's direction. 'And you, sir?' he asked courteously.

'My name is Landon,' Arnold managed to struggle out. 'I am here to . . . to represent John Torrance.'

From someone there came the short hiss of surprise; in Fredericks's features there was no hint other than a sudden contraction of the eyelids. Again there was a short silence. 'I'm afraid I don't quite understand, Mr . . . Landon. CADS is here represented by Mr Dorset and Mr Barclay. I understand that as senior executives of the company they will be able to negotiate on behalf of CADS. But you say . . . do you mean you represent Mr Torrance in a *personal* capacity?'

Arnold's tongue almost clove to the roof of his mouth. 'Yes, sir.'

Fredericks persisted. 'Does this mean that I detect a suggestion that the interests and wishes of CADS as a company might not . . . represent the *personal* wishes of its head, Mr Torrance?'

Arnold's hands were trembling slightly. Unable to speak, he inclined his head. Andre Chevalier was watching him carefully, and now he leaned forward, whispered something to the chairman, and after a short silence during which he observed Arnold thoughtfully, Sir Charles Fredericks slowly nodded. 'All right, Mr Landon. It may be that the personal . . . ah . . . issues may emerge in due course. I think, then, we can begin. Mr Dorset, would you like to make an opening statement?'

Arnold observed the hint of annoyance that flashed over Barclay's narrow features when Dorset was called upon to speak; it was swiftly controlled as Dorset leaned forward to outline the negotiations that had already taken place in Paris, between CADS, Anchédin and Chevalier. He went on, in a well-paced speech, to emphasize the need for swift decisions.

'The fact is, gentlemen, the signs are that by 1990 gallium arsenide chip production is likely to reach two billion dollars, fast catching up on silicon. The chip remains expensive — it costs a hundred times more than silicon — but this will fall dramatically as production increases. We've solved the temperature and insulation problems; all we need now is swift action, early decisions, because we all know it's not just a matter of replacing silicon: it's the use we can make of the new chip in new products. Products both in government and consumer circles; products which we must be involved with if we are to stay ahead of the field.'

'I understand,' Chevalier said smoothly, 'that your competitors in the States have already started to speed up their research programmes.'

'That's right — notably in the field of DBS.' When Sir Charles raised his eyebrows, Dorset added hurriedly, 'Direct broadcasting by satellite.'

'An activity Europe is becoming more and more interested in,' the chairman said, nodding.

'And the Japanese expect to have a mainframe computer running on the new chips within eighteen months,' Barclay intervened. 'They'll be fifth-generation computers, which will be able to talk to each other and take instructions in human written and spoken language instead of the special computer languages . . .'

In spite of himself, Arnold found his mind drifting away from the presentation. As the voices droned on he thought of John Torrance and his view of the past, a distant past which in essence was not far removed from Arnold's own view. But where did Arnold's views fit into this high technology world, where everything seemed possible? He and Torrance were agreed, but how could their attitudes be maintained in such a society?

'We mustn't forget that we're also talking about people,' Arnold suddenly blurted out.

Dorset had been speaking. At the interruption he stopped, turned a puzzled face in Arnold's direction. Castle grunted, as though he was just waking up, and Sir Charles Fredericks stared at Arnold. 'I beg your pardon?'

'People,' Arnold gurgled, unable to say more.

The silence was heavy, almost expectant, but as the slow flush stained Arnold's face, the chairman turned back to Dorset. 'I'm sorry . . .'

'I was just winding up, Sir Charles, to point out that the merger will also be necessary to produce the kind of financial backing and industrial muscle to develop the most exciting possibility of all: the powering of computers by light, produced by the gallium arsenide chip. The chip's light-emitting qualities are already used in lasers and other optical devices; they're already being used in fibre optic cables. But if we can develop our research programmes . . .'

Arnold felt the flush of humiliation remain with him. It had been a mistake to allow himself to be persuaded by John Torrance to attend this meeting. He was out of his depth, scientifically, tactically, indeed, in every way he could think of. He felt thoroughly miserable.

The door opened, after a discreet knock. Conversation ceased. Sir Charles glared at the grey-suited man at the door.

'A message, Sir Charles. Urgent. For Mr Landon.'

'*For whom?*'

'Mr Arnold Landon, sir.'

An angry nod allowed the man entry. The thick envelope lay in Arnold's hands; he stared at it as the messenger withdrew. Dorset was speaking again, summing up, and the noise of the envelope being torn open made him stumble again in his speech. Arnold's fingers were shaking in embarrassment as he drew out the folded sheets and perused them. His heart began to beat irregularly as his mouth went dry, and his stomach began to churn unpleasantly. The papers were from Bewley and Scott, Torrance's stockbrokers. They contained a list of the share-dealings that had taken place during the last two weeks. And they contained the name of the man who had been trading in the shares.

Puzzled, Arnold raised his head, and stared around him, at Sir Charles Fredericks, at Dorset, Chevalier, Barclay, Andrew Castle. He *was* out of his depth. The information surprised him. He had no idea how he could use it.

'Bad news, Mr Landon?' Sir Charles asked, concern injected in his tone.

'Er . . . aagh . . .' Arnold replied. Fredericks stared at him, politician's sympathy evaporating under businessman's impatience, and then he turned to Dorset. 'Thank you for your presentation; You've outlined the needs and the pressures admirably. I think I can speak for my firm, Anchédin, when I say there will be support for your merger proposals. Similarly, if my discussions with Andre are anything to go by . . . ?'

'We will be in support of the proposals,' Chevalier said, smiling faintly, 'on the right terms, of course.'

'And CADS, in the persons of Mr Dorset and Mr Barclay, have made the presentation, so it looks as though we can proceed to—'

'No,' Arnold said.

'I beg your pardon?' Sir Charles Fredericks said, ice entering his tone.

'*No*,' Arnold insisted, finding his courage out of stubbornness. 'We can't proceed to anything. Not yet. Not until some questions are answered.'

'At this stage,' Paul Dorset intervened smoothly, 'all we are discussing is points of principle. The agreement we make on merger today—'

'Sir Charles,' Arnold interrupted boldly. 'Are you aware that over the last ten days or so there have been significant dealings in CADS shares, prior to but also coincident with the accident to Mr Torrance?'

There was a short silence. Sir Charles frowned. 'Dealings in shares are never static—'

'I said *significant* dealings,' Arnold interrupted. 'And I am here on Mr Torrance's behalf to draw attention to them.'

Sir Charles's face was still; there was nothing to be read in his eyes or his tone as he said, 'You've chosen to raise this matter at a critical point, Mr Landon. We are about to conclude a . . . concord on the merger negotiations of three powerful companies, with EEC backing in the wings. You raise the issue of share-dealings. Do I gather from your action you think it should have some influence over the issue of merger?'

'Yes.'

Sir Charles's eyes narrowed suddenly. 'From which, I gather, John Torrance will be . . .'

'*Totally opposed to the merger.*'

There was a sigh. It came from Chevalier, leaning back in his chair as though suspicions had been confirmed. He glanced at Fredericks and shrugged; the chairman caught the movement and hesitated. 'It was John Torrance who actually *started* all these negotiations.'

'He's changed his mind.'

'As everyone is entitled to do. But for what reasons?'

'Because . . . because he now sees things in a different light,' Arnold stumbled, suddenly unsure of himself. 'Because . . . because of what's been happening.'

'The share-dealings?' Sir Charles suggested softly.

'Among other things,' Arnold struggled. 'So many things, unexplained things . . .'

'But you have certain information. I would guess. All right, what is it?'

Arnold took a deep breath. 'Mr Torrance was afraid that any share-dealings would jeopardize the merger talks, because you and M'sieur Chevalier would assume CADS executives were out to make a personal killing, with the result that EEC support would be withdrawn.'

Fredericks frowned, puzzled. 'But that's *illogical*. If Mr Torrance is against the merger, why should he be worried that these talks might fail because of clandestine share-dealings ?'

'But that anxiety on his part arose before he had finally decided against the merger. Later—'

'He had another anxiety?'

Arnold swallowed hard. 'He guessed the share-dealings were started because he had only a twenty-eight per cent share in CADS, and this would be an attempt to oust him from control of the company, and a major voice in the merger proposals.'

Sir Charles stared at him, considering. 'And you, I presume, now know who was behind the dealings in this . . . presumed takeover of power in CADS.'

'Yes.'

'So who was it?'

Shakily, uncomprehendingly, Arnold said, 'Andrew McNeil Castle.'

3

An adjournment for a few minutes was agreed while coffee was served. It came in small, elegant cups. Arnold sipped his miserably, not yet certain where he was going, yet with stirrings at the back of his mind as he flickered surreptitious glances around the hostile room. Of them all, it was only Castle who seemed relatively unconcerned. He lounged back in his chair, his scalp shining under the stubborn tufts of red-grey hair, his petulant mouth confident, his stubby fingers spread on the table in front of him. His piggy eyes flickered only briefly over Arnold, and they held contempt, the kind of dismissiveness Arnold had been aware of the first day they had met, in the library at Oakham Manor.

Paul Dorset seemed lost in thought, his glance directed to his strong hands, clenched in his lap. Barclay was nervous, unable to keep still, tapping his spoon on the table edge. Chevalier gave the appearance of unconcern, but there were angry shadows deep in his eyes, and Sir Charles Fredericks was clearly ruffled, as he waited until the tray had been taken from the room by the waitress.

'If we may begin again, gentlemen. Mr Castle . . . if what Mr Landon says is true, you have not been here with us under a totally honest flag.'

Castle shifted comfortably, and smiled. 'I have to say, Sir Charles, that I *have* now acquired considerable interests in CADS. To that extent, perhaps using my *future* possible interests in the company as a claim to entry here today was — shall we say — a mistake. But my presence here now is clearly OK, because I hold a stake in CADS and I would wish to vote in favour of merger. As for Mr Landon's remarks about shuffles within the company, that's rubbish. I saw this as a straight business possibility. There's no need for anxiety among our European friends; there's going to be no blood-letting, and no battening on CADS by greedy shareholders committed to making a killing. I have an ongoing interest in the company, believe me.'

'We're grateful for the assurance,' Sir Charles said drily. 'Mr Landon, I detect no reason, in spite of the . . . ah . . . rather unusual circumstances, to hold up the voting. I speak for Anchédin when I say I detect nothing *untoward* in this acquisition of shares. Even if it were to topple Mr Torrance, and of that we have no evidence.'

'But where did Castle get the inside information that led him to trade in these shares?' Arnold asked.

Castle scratched himself on the chin and smiled, self-satisfaction oozing from every pore. 'All businessmen move on hunches. I met the people of CADS at Oakham Manor, I *detected* something in the air. So I headed for the stock market. It's called being . . . entrepreneurial.'

Arnold was massively unconvinced but Sir Charles appeared satisfied. Desperately Arnold said, 'There was a fiddle of some kind going on. John Torrance told me—'

'Sir Charles—' Paul Dorset was leaning forward. 'If I may be permitted a word?'

'If it helps clear things up.'

'I think it will, in a sense.' Dorset took a deep, theatrical breath. 'This issue raised by Mr Landon, who is, of course, inexperienced in the tactical manoeuvrings that can go on in the best-run companies, is a rather large red herring, distracting us from the business in hand. It merely confirms for

170

me, since it's Mr Torrance who put Landon up to it, that John Torrance has lost the capacity to take CADS where it needs to go.'

There was a short silence. The chairman glanced at Arnold and then nodded to Dorset. 'Go on.'

'CADS has reached a critical stage in its growth,' Dorset continued. 'I won't bore you with the difficulties it faces in the States; I'll merely admit to them. The European merger was an obvious step, given the nature of the problem, and it produces the most exciting prospects of development imaginable, making CADS part of a massive business empire. But what has become apparent over the last few weeks is that the hand at the helm is no longer as steady as one would wish.'

Chevalier's head raised; there was an almost wolfish glint in his eyes. 'Just what are you saying, my friend?'

'I realize you hold John Torrance in high regard,' Paul Dorset said hurriedly, 'but I think in all honesty you have also been aware of his lack of crispness in the matter of the merger.'

Chevalier hesitated, he glanced at Sir Charles Fredericks. 'I have detected . . . a certain surprising lack of commitment. The heartbeat was . . . missing.'

Arnold felt cold. He stared at Chevalier, and then at Barclay, impassive and stony-faced, as Paul Dorset went on. 'It isn't easy to be critical of a man one has worked with for many years; the more so when it was that man's vision which actually created the company. But the fact remains, and it stares us in the face. John Torrance began to lose grip of the company eighteen months ago. It accounted for some of our problems in the States, in fact. And it accounts for some of his behaviour — his *erratic* behaviour — here in England.'

'How do you mean?' Fredericks asked.

'Cancellation of important meetings, such as the Paris one. Sudden decisions, no explanations to close colleagues, a growing interest in mediaevalism which seemed to be greater than his interest in the company. I've spent most of my working life with CADS and it holds my future. But I guessed that

Torrance was breaking up; I saw the signs and so did others.' He hesitated, waited. Beside him Barclay remained stony-faced. 'And the final irrational decision Torrance has taken is demonstrated here today. It's shown in the presence of Mr Landon who knows damn all about the business. And yet he's here to vote against a merger that will make CADS and its colleagues a major business force in the Western world!'

Sir Charles Fredericks waited for a little while, his eyes flickering from Dorset to Arnold. But it was to Peter Barclay that he spoke. 'Perhaps you would like to give us *your* . . . views.'

Stiffly, grindingly, Peter Barclay's head came up. He seemed unwilling to speak and his face was pale. He was clearly reluctant to say anything that might be seen to be sup-portive of Paul Dorset, his rival for the leadership of CADS if Torrance were ousted, yet when the words came Arnold was shocked by the critical nature of them. 'It became apparent to me some weeks ago that Mr Torrance's heart was no longer in the company. His attention was wandering. His age . . . he is seventy, after all.'

'Wisdom,' Fredericks said softly, 'is not the monopoly of the young.'

'Neither is energy and commitment,' Barclay replied harshly. 'But John Torrance showed none of these qualities.'

Arnold, disturbed, leaned forward with a surge of anger. 'But John Torrance built the company, and made you and Dorset!'

'He's becoming senile,' Barclay said. 'He dreams of the past, an almost primitive past now, when he was building the company up. Those days are past. His day is past.'

'But—'

'Mr Landon.' It was Andre Chevalier, the elder states-man, the man in whom Arnold had detected some of Torrance's own qualities. 'This is business we're talking about.'

Unwillingly Arnold stared at him as slowly, reluctantly, he began to understand. They sat there, these men, executives in their powerful companies, glaring at him because he had introduced irrelevancies into their calculations, irrelevancies that one of their own kind, John Torrance, had suddenly come to appreciate. They sat there, the two rivals; the men they would negotiate with in a cutthroat competitive business; and the man who would bring in vast EEC and government funding to support them. They each held their own interests, their own power, and yet they were now all united against him, and John Torrance. The word crept in, unbidden. He shook his head. 'No, it's not business. It's conspiracy.'

The word seemed to hang in the air, menacing them all. The impact of his statement struck them sharply. Chevalier's head went back slightly, Barclay put down his spoon with a nervous, chinking sound, and something grumbled deep in Andrew McNeil Castle's stomach. Sir Charles Fredericks glared at Arnold unwinkingly as the seconds ticked past. At last Paul Dorset cleared his throat and said firmly, 'I think we should proceed to business, Sir Charles.'

'I agree. We're getting somewhat . . . emotive.' The smooth politician manner took over. 'Gentlemen, I have been made aware that Mr Torrance's proxy will vote against merger. It remains to be determined whether that will materially affect the issue. I foresee little difficulty in support from Europe, from Anchédin and—'

'And Chevalier,' the Frenchman agreed. 'So the stake-holdings in CADS become critical, from your own internal point of view. Mr Torrance, through his proxy, will vote against to the extent of twenty-eight per cent, but without going into details—'

'I have managed to acquire,' Castle said smugly, 'some twelve per cent stake in CADS. Not yet paid for, of course, but registered—'

'And the holdings I have . . .' Dorset said, and paused.

Reluctantly Barclay added, 'Together with mine . . .'

'Should enable us comfortably to push through the vote,' Dorset finished.

'Conspiracy,' Arnold said quietly, again.

'Really, Mr Landon—' Sir Charles Fredericks turned to him, exasperated — 'that kind of remark—'

'I'm not a businessman,' Arnold said slowly. 'I admit it. And I've been told that businessmen hold different kinds of views of ethical considerations from normal people. But I never thought that included this kind of cover-up.'

'I don't know what you're talking about, Mr Landon.'

'I'm talking about murder, Sir Charles.'

* * *

In the stunned seconds that followed, Arnold's mind raced over the whole parade of events of the last weeks, from his first arrival at Oakham Manor. He was appalled by his own boldness, the impulsiveness of his statement, yet though he was yet unable to perceive how the pieces of the jigsaw fitted, the attitudes in this room during the last half hour seemed to crystallize in his mind the probability of conspiracy. For they were all behaving slightly out of character: Dorset and Barclay would inevitably be locked in bitter rivalry, yet today were mutually supportive; Chevalier, who should have been disturbed by Castle's share-dealing activity, had raised no arguments; each supported the other, seeking no advantage. It was not businesslike; it held germs of guilt.

It was Sir Charles who was first to recover. 'Mr Landon. You seem to have an enormous capacity to make alarming statements unsupported by any evidence whatsoever. What the hell are you talking about — murder!'

Arnold's throat was dry. 'Just that, Sir Charles.'

The chairman waved a dismissive hand. 'Really—'

'A man died at Oakham Manor. In a chamber, hundreds of years old. He was murdered.'

Andrew Castle gurgled in surprise. 'At Oakham? I've not heard—'

'This is fantasy,' Chevalier murmured. 'Sir Charles—'

'No, no,' Fredericks said impatiently, 'let's hear this nonsense out and then we can get on. What's this all about, Landon?'

'I — together with John Torrance — discovered a walled chamber at Oakham, used by monks hundreds of years ago. I think a man called Enright was murdered there.'

'Why?'

'He was an electronic engineer.'

'That's hardly a reason for murder,' Fredericks said sarcastically.

'He had with him a listening device, a tape recorder. He was making use of a peculiarity of that chamber. It's possible in that room to hear everything that goes on in a room up above — the one used by John Torrance as the nerve-centre of his business operations while he was at Oakham.'

'So?'

'So he was killed for that information.'

'This is preposterous,' Chevalier snapped angrily. 'What on earth this has to do with our meeting today I can't understand. Sir Charles, do we have to listen to this?'

Fredericks raised a warning hand. 'Hold on . . . Go on, Landon.'

Desperately Arnold shook his head. 'That's it. I really don't know where I go from there. All I know is, there's something wrong in this room today, and Enright died at Oakham, I'm convinced of it.'

Paul Dorset intervened silkily. 'You may be convinced of it, but do I detect some doubt, in the sense that you maybe can't prove it?'

'There's a bloodstain, and I found a piece of tinfoil—'

'But as I recall, Enright was found some miles away, in a ditch.'

'He could have been carried there. The killer wouldn't want it known that Enright died because of what he'd taped down there.'

'What had he taped?' Castle asked curiously.

'Phone calls that John Torrance made to Boston advisers concerning his doubts regarding the merger, and the likelihood that he would pull out of the deal.'

There was a short silence. Sir Charles Fredericks glanced around the room. He nodded slowly. 'That kind of . . . early information would certainly have been useful to everyone here today, I would have thought. I mean, you, Dorset, and you, Barclay, you'd detected a certain disaffection in John Torrance's attitude, but had he ever told you he was against the merger?'

Dorset shook his head. Stiffly Barclay said, 'He hadn't.'

'And Andre,' Fredericks asked smoothly, 'you detected no heartbeat in the negotiations, but did you know Torrance would go against the merger in the end?'

'No.'

Fredericks's glance dwelled on the Frenchman for a moment, then he turned back to Arnold. 'All right, so you suppose that this man Enright died because of information he'd taped. But how did Enright get there in the first place? Didn't you say you and Mr Torrance discovered the chamber?'

Arnold nodded. 'That's right. And we thought it was our secret, since neither of us told anyone about it. But we were both being somewhat . . . naive.'

'You mean someone else could have found out about it?'

'Sir Charles—' It was Barclay's turn to expostulate. 'I'm not at all certain why you should wish to pursue these meanderings from Landon.'

But as he stared at Sir Charles Fredericks, Arnold knew. He was different from everyone else in the room in one respect. Like them, he was a businessman, with an important stake in Anchédin, but he was also a politician. He had intended to bring Anchédin into the merger, but he had also intended to use his influence as a Euro MP to raise government and EEC support for the research and development programmes, which could run to millions. It was why he had reacted sharply to the word conspiracy; he reacted, but could dismiss it. Murder was something else. He had never been touched by scandal in his personal or professional dealings. This was different. Now, he waved a hand to silence Barclay.

'Someone else could easily have found out about it,' Arnold explained. 'I told you, we were naive. Neil Bradon certainly knew about it: he spoke to us in the courtyard when we were going down to the kitchens, to the entrance of the chamber. When we broke in, John Torrance had to go for a torch: it was Peter Barclay who gave him one. Both men could have followed up a natural curiosity, and found what we'd been up to.' Arnold hesitated. 'There was also someone else hanging about in the courtyard after we'd left our discovery. Whoever it was could have gone down to the kitchens, followed in our footsteps.'

'Who else was at Oakham Manor at the time?'

Arnold thought for a moment. Slowly he said, 'Mr Castle . . . and Mr Chevalier, later . . .'

Chevalier exploded suddenly, in a torrent of excited French. After a few moments he collected himself, glared angrily at Arnold and said, 'You're not seriously suggesting I had anything to do with the death of this man Enright!'

'I didn't suggest anything,' Arnold said in reply, but immediately turned back to Fredericks. The room was angry, the atmosphere bristling with hostility, but Fredericks was like a cool rock, his gaze fixed on Arnold. Suddenly they were allies, seeking the truth, the politician for his purposes, Arnold for John Torrance. And Arnold's own, confused thoughts needed the prompting of Fredericks's questions, like a lawyer establishing a case.

'So,' Sir Charles Fredericks pondered, 'someone who knew about the chamber, and who had discovered its . . . ah . . . echoing qualities, decided to place Enright there, to eavesdrop on whatever John Torrance might be saying in private.' He paused. 'And it could have been someone in this room.'

'The likelihood is that it *was* someone in this room.'

'But why was Enright then killed?'

Arnold considered the matter. 'Maybe things went wrong . . . If we assume Enright was acting in a professional capacity, it's likely the police will be able to discover who employed him. It shouldn't be too difficult; he'll have left *some* traces. As to why he was killed, well, maybe he got greedy.'

'How do you mean?' Fredericks asked.

The silence was strained as Arnold hesitated, his mind flickering over the possibilities. 'Well, I suppose what could have happened was that down in the chamber Enright heard the conversations held by Torrance and began to realize he could make more money out of the deal than he'd arranged for. Perhaps he thought the information was worth a lot more, and when he was joined by the man who employed him perhaps they had an argument over money. Maybe there was a struggle . . .' Arnold paused again, looked directly at Sir Charles Fredericks, saw the movement, the encouragement, deep in his eyes and blurted out, 'If we can only point the police to the man who employed Enright maybe we'll find his killer!'

'*No!*'

The word seemed to echo in the room long after the silence had settled; it fluttered in Arnold's mind as he stared at the man who had spoken. Peter Barclay's eyes were flaring with bitterness and anger; his face was pale, his lips stretched in a vicious grimace as he looked about him, eyes darting, a flickering snake tongue seeking revenge. 'No, dammit, I'm not getting saddled with this!'

'*You* employed this man Enright?'

There was a long moment of hesitation, and then Barclay nodded. 'It was I who made the contact.'

It was Sir Charles Fredericks who finally broke the long, tense silence. His cold eyes were fixed on Barclay as he said, 'I seem to detect some *nuance* in the remark. You were the man who made *contact?*'

Peter Barclay's glance flickered towards the tall windows, as though he were contemplating a running jump to the haven of the distant St Katharine Docks. He was already regretting his panicked outburst, but it was too late to retreat.

'Yes. I made the contact. But I didn't pay Enright. And I didn't kill him.'

'Sir Charles, it seems to me we are discussing things of no consequence whatsoever to this meeting.' Andre Chevalier had straightened in his chair, all casual indolence gone as he placed both hands on the table in front of him. 'I really must protest—'

Fredericks cut him short with a gesture. The Euro MP's eyes were cold and glittering. Matters had taken an unexpected turn with Arnold's intervention, and the story had to be pursued. The politician, not the businessman, was uppermost. 'You said, Mr Barclay, that while you made the contact with this man Enright, you did not employ him. So who did?'

Peter Barclay attempted a smile but it came out as a canine grimace, a mixture of threat and alarm. 'I'm not getting saddled with this thing. I've kept quiet, but that's all I've done. Landon was right: the chamber was an open secret, and those two, they were naive if they thought otherwise. And yes, I went in there, and I realized what they apparently did not: that it provided a sounding device that could be used to advantage.' He looked around the table vaguely, as though dreaming of missed opportunities. 'But I also knew that I needed support, needed backing. I had seen the signs, the way Torrance was cooling towards the merger. And I knew I could succeed Torrance, with the right backing. I . . . I found it in Paris.'

Andre Chevalier expelled his breath noisily. He shook his head, reached into his pocket for a cigar case. He lit the cigar in a room which waited silently and expectantly, but his hands trembled gently. 'You're a fool, Barclay.'

'No,' Fredericks said coolly. 'Just a coward, it would seem. So, Andre, you backed Barclay in an attempt to discover not only what Torrance intended doing, but also *when* he decided to act?'

Carelessly Chevalier waved his cigar. 'It's not uncommon business practice, to use subterfuge to discover another's plans. You've done it yourself, Sir Charles — even if you've never been caught . . . Yes, I was worried about Torrance's attitude myself, and when Barclay approached me I agreed to help him. I told him I would support him if he brought information to me — and we agreed upon this man Enright. But if you think I had anything to do with his death . . . I was a long way away when the man died.'

'We . . . I never even saw him after the first few days,' Barclay said hurriedly. 'He just disappeared. I didn't tell Chevalier immediately, but I guessed he'd realized the importance of what he'd taped — Torrance's phone calls to the States — and had lit out, maybe hoping to sell the information elsewhere. But nothing seemed to happen, and then the police called, asked us about Enright. I *had* to keep quiet.'

'As did I,' Chevalier said smoothly, his aristocratic features marked with a feeling of distaste. 'It would have led to recriminations, and destruction of our intentions regarding the merger.'

There was a long silence. The pale blue smoke from the cigar drifted slowly upwards, until it collected like a hazy band near the chandelier above Chevalier's head. Sir Charles Fredericks stared at his hands, as though uncertain how to proceed. At last he turned towards Arnold Landon, the outsider, the man untainted by doubtful business ethics and the chicanery of corporate activity. 'Well, Mr Landon?'

Desperately Arnold's mind clicked over the facts: the electronic engineer Enright had been placed in the chamber by Barclay and Chevalier in an unholy alliance. But they claimed they knew nothing about his death and it would seem they had *gained* nothing from his death. So who had? There was only one person, he realized; one person who, like others at Oakham Manor, could have come into possession of the 'open secret', and who had indeed spent time at the Manor and had had opportunity to discover it. One person who had in fact *acted* upon information regarding John Torrance's intentions.

He stared, fascinated, at Andrew McNeil Castle.

The little fat man was sweating. He pulled at a handkerchief in his breast pocket and mopped at his mouth; his piggy eyes flickered scared glances around the table, as though he was seeking a friend, searching for a support that was lacking. His vision was dimmed with fear, and when he finally held Arnold's glance he almost started in his seat. 'Why are you looking at me?' he asked hastily, his voice croaking with panic. 'What's the matter with you?'

'Mr Castle,' Arnold said quietly. 'It was you who was responsible for all the share-dealing after Enright died. It was you who had the necessary information, gleaned from the tape that Enright had recorded of Torrance's phone calls to his advisers. It was you who—'

'Now wait a minute!' Andrew McNeil Castle held up a flabby, terrified hand. He had seen himself as a shark in his business dealings, surrounded by scavenger fish, but that image was rapidly disappearing. He shook his head. 'This . . . these accusations . . . I don't know what you're implying. All I did was to use some information—'

'Which you got from Enright,' Sir Charles Fredericks intoned.

'You've got it wrong! Look, all I did was to *use* information . . . all I wanted was a piece of the action. It's you characters around this table who are the *businessmen*, the wheeler-dealers! Chevalier there — how the hell do you know you can trust that French bastard? He could have killed Enright for his own twisted reasons. Maybe Enright was blackmailing him, wouldn't give him the information. And Barclay — how come he's suddenly all trustworthy, when he's already admitted to setting the thing up with Chevalier? You crack down on *those* two bastards, not on me. All I did was a bit of share-dealing.' He glared angrily in Arnold's direction as though it was he who was responsible for the destruction of his future, the sinking of his island in the stream. 'You got it wrong!'

'All I pointed out was—'

'I know what you goddamned pointed out and I resent the . . . the implications behind it. Hell, I'm sick of this whole

181

thing; all I wanted was a decent profit, a chance to break into the big time.' His tongue flickered nervously around his rubbery lips, tasting the brine of failure. 'Why don't you ask other questions? What about the way John Torrance never set up his successor; what about the way he let Barclay and Dorset bleed over the years, trying to get the inside track; what about the way these two Torrance aides always tried to get the edge over each other? What about those questions? Because do you really think I got that information by myself? You really think I — a pot-gutted backwoodsman with no real business experience — could have pushed through the share deals without some backing? I didn't get that bloody information myself. *He* got it for me! *He* came and told me there was a way to get in, to grab a good stake in CADS, and rake in from a hell of a European investment, if I simply agreed to one price: my support in due course for his chairmanship of the company within the merger with Chevalier and Anchédin! They're all the same, these bloody company piranhas! They'll snap each other and bloody the water to feed themselves fat! But I'm not like that, and I'm taking no rap for any bastard around this table! I was just acting as a front man. You used the word conspiracy, Landon, but they were *all* conspiring, all negotiating for position. And keeping their mouths shut when things went wrong. But let's get it absolutely clear. *He* was the bastard who was setting me up, so ask *him* where the information first came from!'

They all stared at the man to whom he pointed, dramatically, and over Paul Dorset's face there flickered a shadow dark as death.

4

In the late afternoon the lake was placid, shimmering under the pale sunlight. A coot scuttered across the calm surface, disturbed by a water-rat or vole, and across the meadow a pair of wood pigeons echoed their call, throbbing to each other in the warm afternoon silence. Arnold Landon made his way past the rhododendron bushes for a final walk around the Oakham estate with a feeling of regret; he would have liked to spend longer, search longer, but duty called him back to Morpeth.

Later, when he walked into the main hall of Oakham Manor the servant who greeted him told him that Miss Vallance was in the library. It seemed an appropriate place for him to make his goodbyes. When he tapped on the heavy oaken door and entered, however, he was somewhat taken aback to find she was not alone.

The three of them were standing near the far mullioned window as though enjoying the view, but Arnold realized they were contemplating matters other than Oakham pastures as he recognized the man turning to glare at him. Detective Inspector Carter was still wearing his faded blue suit, and his hair bristled as angrily as ever as Arnold saw the stain of the old arrogance in his eyes. He stared now at Arnold, twisting his bad-tempered mouth. 'Bloody amateurs,' he said.

'I beg your pardon?'

'I said bloody amateurs! Your arrival is just on time, Mr Landon. I was just telling Miss Vallance and Mr Bradon that you didn't tell me everything you knew when you could have. I had a feeling at the time. I knew you was a feller to be watched.'

'I'm not sure—'

'You didn't tell me about the passageway. You held up the investigations. And you must have guessed the reasons for Enright leaving you so abruptly at the pub breakfast table — he'd realized you were at the Manor, where he was scheduled to work that night! And in that passageway, there was the smoke you sniffed, and the tinfoil . . . You was too close, Mr Landon, not open enough. We could've wrapped the thing up if we'd only known. As it was, only when we could prove it was Enright's blood in the corner did they crack—'

'It *was* blood, then?'

Detective Inspector Carter sniffed ungraciously. 'Aye. And when we shoved it at them they started babbling, blaming each other. We got it sorted out now. Most of it like you said to Sir Charles Fredericks.'

'So Chevalier and Barclay employed Enright—'

'And Dorset got wind of the passageway, went down, found Enright there and there was a bit of a struggle. Dorset claims it was an accident: says Enright came for him in a panic, swinging a torch. He hit him. Powerful lad, is Dorset. Enright went down, struck his head. That was it. Dorset, cool bastard, he listened to the tape then, before he did a damned thing more. Then, in the early hours, he lugged the corpse out, dumped it in a ditch . . . but there was nothing he could do about Enright's own car, other than try to buy time by driving it into the stream . . .'

'And then he just kept quiet?'

Detective Inspector Carter's eyes grew reflective. 'That's about the size of it. He contacted our friend Castle, of course, after a few days, advised him that things could get shaky in the merger and a judicious buying of shares now could lead to Castle having a nice financial stake in CADS, with Dorset as top man. The trade was: information to Castle so he could buy in, and Castle's support for Dorset when the crunch came — the showdown with Barclay as to who was the leading light.'

'And Barclay?'

It was Neil Bradon who replied. 'I understand you used the word *conspiracy*. In a sense, that's what it was, but it was an unspoken one. Dorset was no fool. He guessed who'd put Enright down there with the tape. He also guessed that Barclay and Chevalier couldn't say a word when their electronic engineer first didn't come up with the goods, and was then discovered *murdered*. To raise a hue and cry would expose their own role in the proceedings, the way they'd tried to get hold of secret information by doubtful means. They didn't know what Enright had got; they didn't *know* who had killed him. But they could guess. And they didn't dare act. So there was an uneasy silence, a waiting, until things were resolved at the merger meeting. They hadn't counted on Torrance — and you — playing a part, and exposing the whole conspiracy of silence.'

'That may well be,' Carter interrupted testily, 'but all that is nothing to do with me. Business shenanigans . . .'

'And Mr Torrance's accident?' Arnold asked.

Carter grimaced. 'Think we can lay that at Dorset's door, too. He might wriggle over the way things happened with that man Enright, but it's another matter when Torrance gets forced off the road, and there's a car with a dented wing . . . Forensic are pretty sure they can tie in Dorset's car with the crash on the motorway. So, all things being equal . . .' He squinted at Arnold unhappily. 'Even so, like I said, if you'd bloody well come clean with me earlier maybe we'd have got this thing sorted out a damn sight faster. So next time, Mr Landon, don't keep your mouth shut. You can help the police by talking to them: don't hinder them.'

* * *

It had seemed best to make no reply, and Arnold had to admit to himself that Carter had a point to make. It was no use arguing that Carter's own attitudes had contributed to Arnold's silence: Carter would never have understood. The detective inspector was a blunt instrument whose bludgeoning should have brought forth the facts, according to his philosophy: the fact that it had not would have been Arnold's fault in his eyes, and not his own. Perhaps, Arnold considered on reflection, the man was right.

Neil Bradon, at least, was in some doubt.

After Carter had gone, he stood near Tina in the library, their shoulders touching, and he smiled at Arnold. 'I shouldn't pay too much attention to that man, Mr Landon. Without you, whatever he claims, he'd still be floundering around at the Red Lion.'

'I'm not sure—'

'I also have a message for you. I saw Mr Torrance this morning. He sends his regards, and his thanks, and hopes you'll be able to visit him again in the not-too-distant future.'

'I need to get back to Morpeth,' Arnold said, 'but maybe at the weekend . . . I assume Mr Torrance won't be too active in CADS in the future?'

Neil Bradon smiled, and glanced sideways at Tina. 'You don't know him as well as I thought. He'll be back in the saddle, though maybe not riding so hard. He told me that now he's got rid of his cunning workmen . . . I didn't quite get that . . .'

Arnold smiled. 'It's something we've discussed.'

'Well, anyway, he will be back, to a very much more refined operation. Less ambitious, slimmer, taking a more sensible slice of the communications cake than was envisaged in the European multi-national.'

Tina nodded, and looked up at him. 'And I'm more inclined to believe he's beginning to understand what Oakham Manor means.'

'That's right,' Neil Bradon agreed. 'She's been winning us over, Mr Landon. Mr Torrance will be negotiating the purchase from Andrew McNeil Castle — who's caught cold over the CADS share purchase, of course.'

'How do you mean?'

'He and Dorset had gambled: buying up the shares, hoping the price would rise before settlement day. It hasn't, in view of the circumstances. He'd hoped to unload some shares, pay off the holdings out of profits. No longer possible — so he's going to be very happy to sell his interest in Oakham.'

'And the idea,' Tina added, 'is that Neil and I run it as a CADS asset, but in a refined, *English* way, as a conference centre, residential weekends, that sort of thing. I'm not *entirely* convinced—'

'But coming round,' Neil laughed.

'Hmmm.' Arnold lowered his head, considering. 'Well, I'm pleased things are working out, and I'm pleased also that Mr Castle is getting his comeuppance. But I have a feeling it will be worse than he anticipates.'

They both looked at him uncertainly. 'How do you mean?' Tina asked.

Arnold took a deep breath, trying to keep the real pleasure out of his voice, anticipating the excitement his words might cause them both. 'Well, it concerns something that's been bothering me for some time. I'd even discussed it with the Senior Planning Officer in Morpeth. You'll recall I turned up a building contract relating to Oakham?'

'I remember.'

'I read it and read it. Something wrong with it, something puzzling me. But I suppose with other things on my mind I just didn't concentrate. But as I was walking around the lake just now, more relaxed, reviewing the startling events of these last weeks, things came into perspective. I knew I'd been puzzling about the wrong things; missing the obvious.'

'Mr Landon, I believe you're teasing me,' Tina said reprovingly.

Arnold grinned. 'The fact is, it wasn't the contract itself I should have been bothering about. Its provenance is sound and its detail accurate. I should have concentrated upon its wording, upon what it meant.'

'Mr Landon—'

'I can recite it by heart, but you can check the original yourself. I was standing by the lake, and I went over the words again, in peaceful, warm silence at the waterside. *This bille endentyd witnesseth that on the Tewesday next after the feste of Seynt Mathie Apostle the fourte yeere of Kyng Henry the Sexte . . .'*

'So?' Tina demanded impatiently.

'You trace your descent from the man named in the building contract. Thomas Wolfard.'

'That's right.'

'The court agreed that ownership passed to his younger brother William in 1424. It destroyed your claim because Andrew McNeil Castle claims descent from *William* Wolfard.'

'We know that,' Bradon said. 'So what's so important?'

'I told Tina before,' Arnold said. 'Parish registers can be changed for family political reasons; pressures can be applied; church incumbents pushed into falsifications. Who knows, after five hundred years, what really went on?'

'But why is the contract so important?'

'It's real, it's original, and it will be telling the truth in a way other documents of a late date may not be. It's a truth you can take back to the courtroom — and it's likely to stand up.'

'But what truth is that?'

Arnold smiled, savouring the moment. *'The fourte yeere of Kyng Henry the Sexte . . .* the fourth year of Henry's reign was 1425. That contract was made between Thomas Wolfard, Richard Bangor and Adam Ambrynge in 1425 — a year *after* Thomas Wolfard is supposed to have died! Take my word for it: the contract is original and will stand up in court. And against what other evidence? Second-hand only! If the contract was made, as it states, in 1425, Thomas was alive a year after William is supposed to have succeeded to the estate. The son of Thomas Wolfard was therefore the heir, not William: he was not posthumous, and the estate had been taken against the real title. That contract provides better evidence than anything Andrew McNeil Castle can provide.'

'And they'll accept it in court?'

Arnold smiled again. 'Even accounting for the innate conservatism of all lawyers, if you were a judge, what would *you* say?'

And a shaft of sunlight lit up the handsome leather bindings on the shelves of Oakham Manor library.

THE END

Thank you for reading this book.

If you enjoyed it please leave feedback on Amazon or Goodreads, and if there is anything we missed or you have a question about, then please get in touch. We appreciate you choosing our book.

Founded in 2014 in Shoreditch, London, we at Joffe Books pride ourselves on our history of innovative publishing. We were thrilled to be shortlisted for Independent Publisher of the Year at the British Book Awards.

www.joffebooks.com

We're very grateful to eagle-eyed readers who take the time to contact us. Please send any errors you find to corrections@joffebooks.com. We'll get them fixed ASAP.